The Sweetheart Deal

candY APPLe books...JUSt for you.
sweet. Fresh. FUn. take a bite!

The Accidental Cheerleader by Mimi McCoy

The Boy Next Door by Laura Dower

Miss Popularity by Francesco Sedita

How to Be a Girly Girl in Just Ten Days
by Lisa Papademetriou

Drama Queen by Lara Bergen

The Babysitting Wars by Mimi McCoy

Totally Crushed by Eliza Willard

I've Got a Secret by Lara Bergen

Callie for President by Robin Wasserman

Making Waves by Randi Reisfeld and H. B. Gilmour

The Sister Switch
by Jane B. Mason and Sarah Hines Stephens

Accidentally Fabulous by Lisa Papademetriou

Confessions of a Bitter Secret Santa by Lara Bergen

Accidentally Famous by Lisa Papademetriou

Star-Crossed by Mimi McCoy

Accidentally Fooled by Lisa Papademetriou

Miss Popularity Goes Camping by Francesco Sedita

Life, Starring Me! by Robin Wasserman

Juicy Gossip by Erin Downing

Accidentally Friends by Lisa Papademetriou

Snowfall Surprise
by Jane B. Mason and Sarah Hines Stephens

The Sweetheart Deal

by Holly Kowitt

SCHOLASTIC INC.

New York   Toronto   London   Auckland
Sydney   Mexico City   New Delhi   Hong Kong

For Craig

Special thanks to David Manis and Ellen Miles.

ISBN-13: 978-0-545-10068-7
ISBN-10: 0-545-10068-2

12 11 10 9 8 7 6 5 4 3 2   10 11 12 13 14/0

Printed in the U.S.A.
First printing, December 2009

Chapter One

Skyler Hanson's palms were sweating.

Mortified, she wiped them off on her green plaid miniskirt, hoping no one at Fashion Club had noticed. Today's fashionista outfit — black newsboy cap, enormous hoop earrings, above-the-knee white socks — was meant to attract attention. Right now, though, she wanted to hide.

She dreaded making speeches. Getting up in front of thirty girls was *not* her idea of fun. Sometimes she secretly wondered if she even fit in with the club. She took it more seriously than others, somehow. She brushed the thought away; *of course* she fit in — she was one of the leading members!

Luckily, no one was looking at Skyler. Everyone was too busy flaunting the charm bracelets and

1

college-girl blazers they'd scored over Christmas break. It was the first meeting of the new year.

"Did everyone have a fab vacay?" Ashleigh Carr, the club president, didn't wait for an answer. In her pin-striped vest, white blouse, and boy-friend trousers, Ashleigh looked like she should be in a Ralph Lauren ad, not a classroom at Longbrook Middle School. Her audience hung on every word.

"As you all know, I'm graduating this year, so we'll need a seventh grader to replace me as club president." Ashleigh brushed back a strand of long, brown hair. "Voting isn't until March, but today we'll meet the candidates."

Skyler swallowed.

Fashion Club president was her dream.

Maya Benitez leaned forward, dripping with brooches, pearls, and gold chains. "No one could replace *you*, Ashleigh. You're a *legend*."

Ashleigh always had people kissing up to her. It wasn't just that her family had moved to Longwood, a Chicago suburb, from California. It was the way she carried herself, tossed her hair back, and wore clothes special-ordered from a Beverly Hills boutique. She even inspired the best rumors: Ashleigh was kicked out of prep school for a class prank; she and her friends had inspired a TV show about rich kids; a teen pop star had a crush on her.

"Let's hear it for Ashleigh," Maya continued, starting a round of applause. Skyler's best friend, Julia, rolled her eyes.

"She *is* the coolest girl at Longbrook," Skyler reminded Julia.

"Maybe, but you'll be an even better president." Julia clipped a baby barrette into her short, brown hair. Skyler loved Julia's kooky fashion sense — the way she mixed thrift-shop finds with designer pieces. Today she wore a blue embroidered Mexican dress and white go-go boots.

"Who wants to give the first campaign pitch?" Ashleigh looked around. A redhead in a frilly headband stood up and walked to the front of the room.

"My name is Blake Tuttle," she said. "And I'm running on an aromatherapy platform."

Skyler and Julia exchanged glances. Blake was a space cadet.

"Girls today have to struggle with a very important question." Blake paused dramatically. *"What's my signature scent?"*

Her voice rose. "Honey and gardenia? Lime and cedar? Autumn leaves?"

Blake's eyes got misty. "Getting dressed doesn't

3

stop with your clothes. The scent of change is in the air! Vote for Blake!"

After a spurt of polite applause, Ashleigh nodded at Skyler. *Her turn!* She picked up her pink paisley portfolio and forced herself to walk to the front of the room.

Deep breath.

She looked back at Julia, and her friend shot her a you-can-do-it look. Skyler tucked her long, butterscotch-colored hair behind her ears and tried to stop her slender frame from shaking. She set the portfolio on the desk.

"Hey." Skyler managed a smile. "I'm Skyler Hanson. I just want to say how much I love being part of this club."

People smiled back, and she realized how much she meant it. Organizing the Frock 'n Roll fundraiser, poster-painting for the clothing drive, modeling in the Teen Chicago fashion show — it had all been a blast. Especially when other parts of school — like algebra — were more of a struggle.

"I want to bring this club to a new level." Skyler's heart was pounding. "Field trips to the Art Institute and Merchandise Mart, shopping trips downtown — we can learn a lot about trends, designers, the history of fashion. Seminars in

4

sewing and design would be cool. And how about a black-and-white ball?"

Her eyes slid sideways to check crowd reaction. Did she sound too teacher-ish and intense? People were smiling, with one exception: Madison Gillette stared at her nails, looking pointedly bored.

Ignoring the snub, Skyler continued.

"I've always believed in the power of fashion." Skyler's voice got stronger. After all, she had pored over *Vogue* to get ideas for Barbie outfits at the age of six. "Coco Chanel said: 'Fashion has to do with ideas, with the way we live.'" She could feel herself getting excited. "So, vote for Skyler! Thank you."

She tried not to race back to her chair. The group applauded warmly, and Julia gave her a thumbs-up. Jameeka Lacewell leaned over and patted her on the back. Sienna Goldblum whispered, "*Go,* girl."

It was over! They liked it!

Big relief.

Now Madison appeared to be counting ceiling tiles. She was a candidate, too. The ash-blond beauty made sure everyone knew what she thought of Skyler's pitch: bo-ring.

"Your turn, Madison," said Ashleigh.

Madison took her time strolling to the front. Paparazzi-ready in a leather jacket with an enormous fur collar, she stopped to wave and blow kisses. Black leggings and high-heeled boots made her legs look extra long. Did she think she was at the Golden Globes? Skyler felt a wave of disgust.

She remembered Madison in third grade, showing off electric sneakers.

"I'm Madison Gillette." She leaned into the audience. "Is it just me, or does Skyler make the club sound like *school*?" Madison wrinkled her nose. "Cut the lights, please."

Cut the lights?

It took Skyler a moment to realize Madison was showing a video on the monitor suspended from the ceiling. On-screen, Madison sashayed down a runway to the beat of pounding rap music. The camera cut to her wearing different outfits: a slinky gold tank; a belted fur vest; a shiny purple party dress.

The room filled with "oooh"s and "aaaah"s.

How had she made such a professional-looking video? "Her father," mouthed Julia. Of course — he made commercials for an ad agency. Madison's voice-over came on.

"Great taste: You either have it or you don't. Vote Madison."

The last shot showed Madison in a pink bubble bath, wearing a tiara and blowing a kiss.

Everyone roared as the lights flicked on. Madison did a coy "Who, me?", hiding in her fur collar while the crowd clapped and stamped their feet.

"Off the hook!" someone yelled, amid whistles and "Woo-woo"s. Skyler clapped along, but she felt deflated. Madison's campaign video was a huge hit.

Rats.

Ashleigh stood up. "You guys rocked," she said. "The election isn't for two months, but it's good to start getting to know the candidates. Next week, we'll talk about the winter fashion show." She looked down at her clipboard. "Before we leave, though, I need someone to do me a favor."

Thirty hands shot up.

"Ashleigh! Over here!"

"Hey!"

"MEEEEE!"

"I pick —" Ashleigh scanned the room, while everyone waited. "Skyler and Madison."

Skyler and Madison exchanged glances. *Together?*

While the other club members pulled on ski jackets and down vests, Ashleigh pulled Skyler and Madison aside. Madison looked just as reluctant as Skyler felt. What was Ashleigh was up to?

"You're both super-persuasive," Ashleigh said. "I need someone to sweet-talk Mr. Brodkey into letting us use his classroom next month for the fashion show. We need a changing room."

Was that it? Skyler tried not to look disappointed at the unglamorous errand. Visiting her math teacher wasn't thrilling, but she was eager to prove herself.

"Done," said Madison.

"No prob," said Skyler.

The two girls walked down the hall without much chitchat. Skyler knocked on Mr. Brodkey's door, unable to see through the window. The glass had been papered over with an algorithm chart, and a poster that read WHAT'S YOUR SINE?

Mr. Brodkey came to the door, raising a bushy unibrow in surprise. He was a hairy guy in a flannel shirt, glasses, and a long, black ponytail. "Skyler, Madison. I didn't know you guys were numbers freaks."

He opened the door wide, revealing a room packed with math geeks. Every single one was staring at them.

"Come in," he ordered.

Chapter Two

Numbers freaks?

Then it dawned on Skyler: This was a Mathletes meeting. She remembered Brodkey describing the team at assembly. "It's an interscholastic math competition," he had said. "Quadratic equations! Variables! Fun stuff!"

The teacher pointed to empty chairs. "Sit."

Madison cut him off. "Love to, can't. We're here to see if Fashion Club could use your room for —"

The words *Fashion Club* brought snickers.

"Oh." Brodkey's unibrow drooped. "Well, stick around for a minute. Meeting's almost over."

Oh, great. Now they were trapped!

Skyler and Madison exchanged horrified looks. Stick around for a . . . *Mathletes meeting*? Skyler could see Madison deciding whether or not to blow it off. They both frowned. Neither wanted to let the other get points with Ashleigh.

"Big props to Madison!" Skyler imagined Ashleigh saying. "She got us Brodkey's room! GIVE HER SOME LOVE!" The club would roar with applause.

Skyler planted a studded hobo bag on a seat in the back row, and sat down. Her rivalry with Madison outweighed her horror of math geeks. Madison sighed and dumped her red patent leather purse on the chair next to her.

A glittery notebook fell out, and Madison grabbed it. Skyler recognized a slam book that had been going around school. People wrote in it anonymously, saying things that were too mean to say to someone's face. Madison opened the book and started writing furiously, flaunting her lack of interest in the scene around her. Well, if she wanted to be snarky, there was plenty of material here.

Turning her head, Skyler took in the view.

Whoa.

She saw white tube socks with clogs, cell phone holsters attached to belts, and a sea of unconditioned hair. The boy next to her wore a black calculator-watch the size of a baked potato.

"These people are freaks," Madison whispered, making a face.

"Shhhhhh," Skyler whispered back.

She had been only dimly aware of Mathletes, classifying such activities as Things of No Interest at Longbrook, along with the Recycling Club, science fair, and Salute to the Metric System assembly. Such events barely existed for her. Fashion Club, Pajama Day, the Valentine's Day Dance — these were the words splashed across Skyler's week planner in purple gel pen.

Skyler recognized a few people. Emily Berman, a spiky-haired, artsy-craftsy oddball who drew vegan-themed comics. Jasper Resnick, a mega-brain who always said, "Are you inputting that?" Adam Dowd, whose glasses were as thick as swimming goggles. A couple of others who belonged to the First-in-Line-to-See-*The-Lord-of-the-Rings* crowd.

At the front of the room, a guy in a tuxedo T-shirt was talking. "Well, we stank at rational numbers," he said. "But in linear equations we're going to *kick butt*."

"Sounds spaz-tastic," Madison whispered.

"I dunno." Skyler shrugged. "It's kinda cool they're so into it."

Actually, the scene was pretty interesting. *We*

go to the same school, but we inhabit a totally different universe, thought Skyler. This world was right under her nose, but it had been invisible to her. Was her world as distant to them?

"Friday is our Pizza Pi party," said a girl in overalls and a tie-dyed thermal top. Skyler automatically gave her a mental makeover. A belted pink dress to make her waist look small, she thought. Over it, a classic black trench coat and matching cotton tights. Short cropped high-heeled boots for height. Dangly silver earrings. A blunt bob haircut with straight bangs.

I'm good, thought Skyler. Inspired, she turned her attention to a guy wearing a *Battlestar Galactica* tee over long sleeves. She chose funky prep for him: a white button-down shirt over a rock band tee, and skater-boy long shorts. She trimmed his hair, rearranged his part, and put him in cool basketball shoes.

Not bad, thought Skyler.

She went around the room, assigning clothes to people. It was like playing with paper dolls. A mini-jumper to show off a petite frame. High-waisted pants to lengthen short legs. A green woven shirt to bring out gray eyes . . .

"That's it. Time for refreshments." Thermal Top Girl interrupted Skyler's thoughts. *Finally!* As the meeting broke up, she and Madison made a beeline for Mr. Brodkey. He was talking to a boy in a shirt that read I LIKE ANGLES — TO A DEGREE.

"Mr. Brodkey!" Skyler and Madison shouted in desperation.

"I'll catch up with you later, Taro." Brodkey turned to them. "How did you like Mathletes? Exciting stuff, huh?"

"Um —" Madison flashed a fake smile. "Totally. We were wondering if Fashion Club could use your room for a —"

"Too bad you missed the Mix 'n Math picnic," he continued.

"Bummer," said Skyler. "On February twenty-fifth, we —"

"I'll look at my calendar." He pointed to the snack table. "Graze."

Skyler and Madison checked out refreshments while they waited. "Even the snacks are nerdy," said Madison, plucking a Bugle chip from a plastic dish. She watched a guy walk by in a Death Star Tech Support T-shirt. "God. What. Losers."

Madison was really starting to bug her.

She and Skyler had a troubled history. At one time, they had been good friends, gossiping and raiding the mall together for free cheese samples. Madison was nicer then, showing her vulnerable side when her parents weren't getting along. It bugged Skyler that her friend turned against people so easily, but she chose to ignore it.

Then, at fifth grade summer camp, Madison turned against Skyler. Everyone in the cabin ignored her — Madison's orders. Skyler was awkward then, tall for her age, and cursed with frizzy hair. Madison branded Skyler as uncool.

After a miserable summer, they finally made up — but never regained the same easy friendship. In the popular crowd, Skyler kept her distance from Madison. "Your frenemy," Julia called her. Madison was too powerful not to have as an ally, but she was too dangerous to be a real friend.

Meanwhile, Skyler grew into her height, straightened her hair, and discovered her inner fashionista. But her stint as a social outcast made her sensitive to people left out of the whirl.

"They're *not* losers." Skyler's voice rose. "They're just fashion-challenged."

"A dork's a dork." Madison spoke firmly. "You can't change that."

"Sure, you can." Now Skyler began to get angry. This was the kind of snobbish attitude that was ruining Fashion Club. "*Everyone* has potential, Madison."

"Yeah, right." Madison popped another Bugle.

"It's true!" Skyler waved a hand around the room. "Pick any guy here. I could make him so fierce, Ashleigh Carr would *beg* him for a Sweetheart Dance on Valentine's Day." The Sweetheart Dance was a turnabout moment at the school Valentine's Day Dance, when for one song, girls asked guys to dance.

Wow — did that really come out of her mouth?

"Really?" Madison raised an eyebrow. "The Valentine's Day Dance is in six weeks."

Skyler had been trying to make a point — not a serious offer. Was it really and truly *possible*? Skyler wasn't sure. If she really believed in the "power of fashion," this was her chance to back it up. She'd have to work fast. "I could do it," Skyler said, trying to muster confidence.

"Anyone?" Madison's eyes lit up.

"ANYONE." Skyler raised her chin.

Madison motioned for Skyler to turn around.

Behind her, a hooded figure in science safety goggles was talking loudly. Long hair peeked out from a purple plastic cape printed with WIZARDS & WARRIORS. A janitor's belt around his waist held a cell phone, PDA, pocketknife, and possibly, a wireless fax. To make matters worse, he was speaking in a fake robot voice.

15

He seemed to have missed several belt loops, so stonewashed jeans bunched up around his waist. Those jeans appeared to be hemmed. On his feet were white socks, stuffed into black leather Viking sandals.

Skyler stood watching, horrified but fascinated. The guy took nerdiness to a whole new level.

"The Green Goblin versus She-Hulk?" he was saying. "Not even CLOSE!"

Madison smiled sweetly.

"I pick *him*."

Chapter Three

Skyler's heart sank. The purple dragon-slayer was off-the-charts geeky. She'd wanted a challenge, not a suicide mission. Now he was performing an elaborate handshake with a guy in a knit cap. They bumped chests, stacked fists, and licked pinkie fingers before linking them.

Good grief.

"Let's make this *really* interesting." Madison pushed up her sleeves. "If you manage to turn this nerd around by Valentine's Day, I won't run for Fashion Club president. If you tank, then *you* don't run. That's how sure I am this guy is hopeless."

This was big.

Being Fashion Club president was important to Madison. And it meant everything to Skyler. "But how do we decide if I've done it?" Skyler wondered what she'd gotten herself into.

Madison thought for a second. "It's like you said: Ashleigh's the test. If she asks him to dance on Valentine's Day, you win. She's always on the lookout for new guys who are cool enough for her. If he catches her eye, that's it."

Skyler gulped. Was she actually going to do this?

Madison sighed dramatically. "Loser Outreach was *your* idea."

Her words set something off in Skyler's brain. At camp that summer, Madison had labeled her like that — the phrase still rang in Skyler's ears. "She's a loser," Madison had announced, ruining her life in a split second. Now, her tone of contempt captured everything that was wrong with middle school. A desire to prove Madison wrong made Skyler's throat tighten. They'd had disagreements before, but —

This one was personal.

"Deal," Skyler said fiercely.

Her eyes locked with Madison's. Skyler nodded again for emphasis, afraid to look back at the super-geek she had just agreed to rescue.

Mr. Brodkey returned with his calendar. "That Thursday? I suppose Fashion Club could use the room." His voice became earnest. "But I hope you'll come back to Mathletes. As we say, 'Come for the fractals, stay for the pita chips.'"

"Thanks," Madison and Skyler said in unison.

"Now if you'll excuse me, ladies," Mr. Brodkey said, "I have to return a polyhedron. . . ." He picked up a soccer ball and wandered off.

"Well?" Madison turned to Skyler and tapped her pink plaid Swatch. "Tick, tick, tick . . ."

Deep breath.

Skyler inched toward the Cape Man, trying to be casual. She reluctantly touched his purple plastic shoulder, and he turned around, startled.

"Uh, hi," she said. "I'm — Skyler."

People around them were staring. The guy in the knit cap snorted.

"Greetings and salutations," said the Cape Man.

"Can we go somewhere and talk?" she asked.

"Sounds intriguing." He glanced at his watch. "But I have Dwarf Quest at four."

"Cool." Skyler had no idea what he was talking about. "This won't take long. Promise."

A bunch of curious Mathletes crowded around. The Cape Man grabbed a backpack the size of a mini-refrigerator. He turned to his friends and said, "If I don't return to the mother ship in five, send someone after me."

19

Skyler guided the boy to the playground steps by his purple plastic elbow. As she sat down next to him, he pulled out a can of bubble-gum soda. "Beverage of the gods." He threw his head back for a giant gulp.

Skyler drew another deep breath.

He drummed on his notebook, making sputtering noises like a record-scratching DJ. "I'm a drummer." His hands moved with surprising speed. "I've got a band."

Skyler nodded. "What's your name?"

"The Vectors," he said.

Skyler realized he had misunderstood the question. "No, not the band — what's *your* name?"

"Nathan Stillman." He continued his solo. Then he seemed to switch between other imaginary instruments: guitar and keyboard.

"Nathan," Skyler began. "I'm not actually a Mathlete."

"You're kidding," he said calmly.

"I've got kind of . . . a weird question."

As he jammed, Skyler fidgeted with her chunky bracelet. What was she doing? Offering a total stranger a makeover suddenly stuck her as presumptuous. But she might as well go for it now.

"I'd like to bring out your potential," she said earnestly.

Nathan looked amused. "My potential for *what*?"

"Your potential to be a cool guy at school." She sounded too *infomercial*.

"Why? I mean, what would *you* get out of it?" He looked confused.

"I like to help people pull their look together." Skyler leaned forward, excited. "It's what I'm good at. I think everyone has —" She corrected herself. "I think you have potential. We could work together to make you a big hit at the Valentine's Day Dance." Better to leave out the part about Ashleigh Carr.

Nathan frowned. "What's the Valentine's Day Dance?"

What? The biggest blowout bash of the year, and he'd never *heard* of it?

This was shocking, but also impressive, in a way. At the cafeteria "cool" table, the Valentine's Day Dance was all anyone talked about — especially what to wear. Glitter tulle vs. red satin, gold lamé sandals vs. black velvet pumps; the discussions were endless. Madison was guarding her choice of dress like a state secret, hoping to make a grand entrance.

If the school's big blowout wasn't on Nathan's radar screen, then he truly went his own way.

"It's the dance of the year," she sputtered.

"Why would I want to go?"

Skyler was speechless. Going to the Valentine's Day Dance was a no-brainer. Everybody went!

"Because it's *fun*," said Skyler, remembering the blast she had last year transforming the gym into a Paris night scene with a giant cardboard Eiffel Tower, a skyline of twinkling lights, and yards of blue silk for the Seine. "Afterward, people have cool parties. Being a hit there would make you popular."

Nathan pondered this a moment. "Why would I want to be popular?" He sounded genuinely curious. "What would I get out of it?"

Skyler was stumped. This wasn't something you normally had to explain. Everyone wanted to be popular, right? Then you could be with other kids who were, uh, popular. Skyler scratched her head.

Images of the "cool" crowd flashed through her mind. Tim Alcoke's spring bash, Madison's rec room, Kyle Townshend playing soccer. The food court at the mall.

"The popular kids sort of . . . rule the school." She plumped the bow on her miniskirt. "They're on committees, they decide things. Who leads drama club, who emcees the Valentine's Day Dance. Stuff like that."

Nathan looked unconvinced.

"Don't you want people to know who you are?" Skyler asked Nathan.

Just then a curly-haired guy in surgical scrubs and giant headphones opened the school door and handed Nathan a plastic bottle labeled FAKE BLOOD. Nathan stood up and high-fived him, then looked down at Skyler.

"The right ones already do," he said.

He was halfway across the playground before she realized the conversation was over.

Chapter Four

Even through the phone, Skyler could hear disbelief in Julia's voice. "Let me get this straight," said Julia. "After Fashion Club, you went to a *Mathletes* meeting?"

Skyler was updating her best friend on the last few hours. She had collapsed on a beanbag chair in her bedroom, which was decorated in retro colors: acid green, hot pink, electric orange. While she talked to Julia, she watched a TV nature show on mute. A mother bobcat was carrying her cub by the skin of its neck. Skyler always found these shows strangely comforting.

"Julia." Skyler squeezed a stuffed monkey. "We really were at a Mathletes meeting. I swear on a stack of *Teen Vogues*."

"Describe," said Julia.

Julia and Skyler had been best friends si
the beginning of middle school, when they n
at Fashion Club. It was hard to believe a year and
a half had passed since the girl in suspenders
and a funky headband asked Skyler if she could
borrow a pen. They became fast friends —
shopping, scheming, whipping up M&M pancakes,
crazy hairdos, and homemade valentines.

They confided in each other about friends,
boys, and the more absurd moments of life in the
"cool" crowd. Julia was more on the fringes of
the group, because of her artsy ways and indepen-
dent streak. Skyler liked talking to her about the
cast of characters; Julia had an interesting take on
people. It helped to know that whatever happened
with the group, they always had each other.

Skyler could hear paper rustling. "What are
you doing?" she asked, stalling for time. She wasn't
eager to tell Julia about the bet.

"Trying to make a bracelet out of buttons,"
said Julia. She was always doing something
creative — sketching fashion designs in her
leopard-print notebook, or remaking an old T-shirt
into a halter. She had even customized her denim
jacket with buttons and gold braid.

"Go ahead — I'm listening," said Julia.

Reluctantly, Skyler told her about the Mathletes meeting and her bet with Madison. Usually Skyler relied on her friend to give her a reality check, and tell her when she wasn't seeing the whole picture. Skyler liked to plunge into something headfirst and ask questions later, while Julia was more cautious. Right now, Skyler wasn't in the mood for her friend's good advice.

Of course, Julia was skeptical.

"Why would you want to take on that guy?" Julia remembered him from history class the year before. "Your cool count could take a total dive. And you could lose your chance to become president!"

Skyler swallowed.

"Maybe I was a little hasty," Skyler admitted. "Madison was really getting to me." The TV screen was now showing a spider spinning a web. "But shouldn't I use my fashion brain for a good cause?" Skyler felt stubborn about it. "I've always wanted to do a makeover."

"Yeah, but —"

"It's what I'm good at," Skyler said. "The guy needs *help*."

"Help is one thing," said Julia. "Overreaching is another."

Skyler tried to see the situation through Julia's eyes. She *had* been impulsive. But when she remembered Madison's snide comments, she felt mad all over again. Skyler felt like she had to prove a point: There were no losers, only people who hadn't found the right clothes.

She should know. She had remade herself from a gawky kid into a cool Fashion Club member. Couldn't she help someone else?

"There," said Julia. "You have my official warning. But if you go through with this crazy idea," Julia took a breath, "I'll give you total support. And a few clothing suggestions . . ."

Skyler hugged the monkey, sighing with relief. Her best friend's backing was crucial.

"Really?" Skyler asked.

"It could be interesting." Julia admitted. "As an experiment. I always think fashion comes from inside, but maybe you *can* show someone how to dress."

"I might not get the chance, anyway." Skyler watched the spider trap an insect. "When I asked him, he turned me down."

"You dodged a bullet," said Julia. "Count yourself lucky."

The next day at lunch, Skyler and Julia were sitting with the usual seventh grade "cool" table crowd: Madison, in a nautical prep blazer; Sienna

Goldblum, a delicate blond who once organized a school scrunchie drive; Jameeka Lacewell, a fierce diva who changed outfits several times a day; and Kyle Townshend, a tall, cute jock in hip-hop gear. Skyler always sat up a little straighter when Kyle was around; like many girls at school, she had a little crush on him. Madison was telling everyone about yesterday's meeting.

"Math nerds." Sienna's blue eyes opened wide. "What was it like?"

"A fashion nightmare." Madison waved her hand. "Black socks with shorts. Prewashed jeans. Calculator watches."

"Ouch," said Jameeka.

"It was torture." Madison sighed. "We couldn't wait to leave."

Skyler felt a twinge of guilt. Laughing at math geeks made her uneasy. Should she defend them? Better not to start up with Madison . . . she decided to let it go.

Tap, tap, tap.

Skyler felt someone's finger on her shoulder. Turning around, she saw science safety goggles and a T-shirt that read KISS MY ASTEROIDS. Nathan!

Madison and Jameeka exchanged glances.

"Gotta go." Skyler got up abruptly, motioning for Julia to follow.

"But I haven't finished my . . ." Julia held up her eggplant burrito. Skyler grabbed Julia's anime athletic bag with an attached whistle. Then Skyler gathered up her own lunch and plaid backpack.

"Who's the . . . ?" Kyle looked at Nathan.

"Bye, guys." Skyler led Nathan away, glancing behind to make sure Julia was coming, too.

"Let's go to my office," Nathan said as they threaded their way through the chaotic lunchroom. Skyler looked at Julia and raised an eyebrow.

He led them to a table at the far end of the cafeteria, motioning for some guys trading Magic cards to clear space. Grudgingly, they slid over, staring at the girls. Skyler had gone French schoolgirl in a white blouse under a tiny gray vest, with black beret and tights. Julia was funky eclectic in layered jerseys and a plaid blazer, long fake pearls and rubber boots — cute with her short, tousled brown hair. Skyler noticed they didn't exactly blend in.

"Nathan, this is Julia." Skyler introduced everyone as they sat down. "Julia, Nathan."

Nathan turned to Skyler, not even noticing Julia's outstretched hand. "I've thought about your offer and I'm willing to make a deal." He played with the zipper on his backpack. "I told you about my band, the Vectors? Well, if you get us a deal to play the Valentine's Dance, I'm in."

29

"Really?" Skyler leaned across the table. "You'll let me make you —" She was about to say, "over," but stopped. "Awesome?"

"Affirmative." Nathan nodded. "Being 'cool' " — he held fingers up to show quotation marks — "could help me get the band gigs. Like you said, school is run by pod people —"

Skyler looked at Julia. "I didn't use those words exactly —"

"— who aren't going to give guys like us a break. So: infiltrate the system and then subvert it." He put his hands behind his head.

"What do you mean?" asked Julia.

"I'll walk the walk." Nathan shrugged. "Till I reach my goal. Then: game over."

This was exciting — but scary. He was agreeing to be her guinea pig! Was she really up to it?

"I'll check. The band for the Valentine's Day Dance is probably already booked," Skyler said, her heart beating fast. "But I can line up another gig." She was almost afraid to look at Julia. "What kind of music do you play?"

"Are you familiar with Der Sfinkter?" Nathan's fingers drummed on the table.

Skyler and Julia looked at him blankly.

"Pus Monkey? Quiche of Death?" Nathan tried. They shook their heads.

"Very cool stuff. We push a lot of boundaries."

"Okay, Nathan." Skyler said finally. She was happy to have a project — and this was a juicy one. "I'll get you a gig. Maybe not the Valentine's Day Dance, but a gig. If you want to have a cool band, though, you have to let me make you cool."

"Meaning . . . ?" His head tilted.

"Everything: clothes, grooming, social life."

"You're scaring me." Nathan pushed up his goggles.

"Trust me," said Skyler. "I can help."

"Let's do it. With great power comes great responsibility." Nathan said, and got up to stretch. "Stan Lee said that."

Once again, Skyler and Julia looked blank.

"Inventor of Spider-Man." He smiled and lifted his chin.

"Cool." Skyler nodded at Julia. "Tomorrow afternoon we get started. Where should I meet you after school?"

"The park. Third chess table."

They all nodded. "Okay," said Skyler.

Skyler's heart pounded. Nathan was all hers to make over! All she had to do now was get the nerdiest guy in school a hot music gig.

No problem.

Chapter Five

"If the Vectors are so great, why haven't I heard of them?" The question came from Hunter Waxman-Orloff, the head of the Student Planning Council. An intense girl with brown, wavy hair and green glasses, she sat at a desk in the student lounge checking yearbook proofs.

"C'mon, Hunter." Skyler sat on her desk, irritated. "Do you know every warm-up band at the Arena?" The Arena was a local concert hall in their Chicago suburb. She was sure the Vectors hadn't played there, but it didn't hurt to mention them in the same sentence.

"Were they at Live Earth in Rio?" a long-haired guy in the corner asked.

"Um, I'm not sure," Skyler said.

Just then, Sienna Goldblum walked into the office. All heads turned to look at the blond beauty in a pink-and-gray boyfriend cardigan, brushing back blond corkscrew curls. She would never admit to not knowing a band.

"Sienna, great news," Skyler tossed out. "We might be able to get the Vectors for the Valentine's Day Dance."

"The Vectors," Sienna repeated, looking blank.

Skyler flipped her hair back. "You know — the band."

"Oh, the *Vectors*," said Sienna, as if finally hearing it right. "AWESOME!" Sienna did *not* disappoint.

Hunter dropped a folder on the table. "The Val Dance is booked. Crushed Popsicle is playing."

Skyler was actually relieved. Though she hadn't heard the Vectors' music, she was sure the Valentine's Day Dance was out of their league. By asking Hunter, she had fulfilled her obligation, and could now dig up a more obscure gig.

"Are there other events that need music?" Skyler looked around the room.

The long-haired guy checked his clipboard. "Student Health Carnival." He handed her a flyer that read IT'S SCIENCE-SATIONAL!

"Cool." Skyler nodded.

Hunter sighed. "I can't deal with this now." She shoved papers into a folder. "I've got year-book proofs, Model UN, and Y-Teens." Hunter was the most overbooked person at school. "Where's their demo?"

This was annoying. Did Hunter really have to hear the band before she booked them for the *Student Health Carnival*?

"The rules say I can't book anyone unless they submit a demo," insisted Hunter.

So the Vectors have to lose the gig because of a stupid rule? thought Skyler. Then she remembered she had a bootleg CD for a college band that Julia had lent her. A little dishonest, but only temporarily — she'd straighten it out later. Who would know? She opened her purse and stuck the disc in the boom box.

A danceable pop tune filled the room. The long-haired guy nodded to the beat.

"Fine, okay, they're in." Hunter looked at her watch. "For God's sake, it's three fifteen." She grabbed a leather briefcase monogrammed with her initials. "Set it up with their manager. No pyro-technics, and they have to bring their own security."

As Hunter flew down the hall, Skyler saluted. *Yes!*

When Skyler left the room, she grabbed Julia by the sleeve of her vintage baseball jacket. "Guess who's playing the Student Health Carnival?"

"Perfect." Julia laughed. "Will Nathan have to dress as a large intestine?"

"Even getting that gig wasn't easy," Skyler explained. "Hunter asked to hear their music and all I had was that college band CD you gave me." She sighed. "You know, Mystery Train? I may have — *somehow* — given the impression that it was the Vectors' demo."

"WHAT?" Julia shook her head in disbelief.

"It's the health carnival." Skyler's voice rose. "They have exhibits like 'Our Friend Saliva'! Who's gonna care?"

"*They* will — when the Vectors show up, instead of Mystery Train." Julia grabbed Skyler's arm. "How do you get yourself into these things?"

Skyler knew Julia was right — but she didn't want to think about it. Skyler always got carried away in the moment, doing whatever it took to serve her agenda. Julia was more practical, thinking ahead and pointing out problems. So what if Skyler had fudged the truth a little? It was for a good cause.

Julia gave her a tragic will-you-ever-learn? look, which Skyler chose to ignore.

"It'll be fine." Skyler led her down the hall. "Let's find Nathan and get this party started."

They walked across the street to McKinley Park, a square-block patch of land with a baseball diamond, tennis courts, and playground. Although patches of snow dotted the ground, people were out enjoying the sunshine. Young moms pushed bundled-up toddlers down the slide, teenagers threw Frisbees, and old men sat on benches.

"Where is he?" Skyler scanned the row of cement chess tables, which were surprisingly packed.

"Over there," said Julia. "The one dressed like a galactic warlord."

Today Nathan was wearing a maroon jacket with silver-winged shoulders. He was deep in negotiations with a· beefy kid in a baseball cap with a lightning bolt. Other kids were gathered around, watching.

"Don't insult my intelligence." Nathan shook his head. "No way is Rat Girl #8 worth more than Tentacle Freaks." On his right was a stack of comic books in plastic sleeves.

Skyler could sense an air of deadly seriousness as they approached the table.

"Au contraire, *mon frère*," said Baseball Cap Guy. "The inker on that was Gary Mendez."

Skyler and Julia edged around the crowd. In her Day-Glo pink-and-silver ski jacket, Skyler felt conspicuous. The guys gave them dirty looks, as though a foreign power had invaded their turf. Nathan, on the other hand, was oblivious to everyone except his trading partner.

"Ten dollars." Nathan leaned back. "Final offer."

Baseball Cap Guy shook his head, disgusted. "Rat Girl travels back in time to rescue the *Titanic*," he argued. "Mint condition."

The two guys on either side of Baseball Cap Guy exchanged tense glances. One was a pony-tailed guy in an army jacket; the other looked like a Secret Service agent, with dark glasses. Behind Nathan stood his own crew: a big-nosed boy in a parka over surgical scrubs, and Jasper Resnick, who had long, straw-colored hair and a wireless radio curled around one ear. With the antennae out, he resembled a Martian.

Most fascinating to Skyler was a girl on the out-skirts of the group — slight, olive-skinned, in a baggy sweatshirt. Her long black ponytail was tied with a plain rubber band, and her backpack had a Batman logo. She kept pushing back blue glasses that were too big for her small face. *About my age*, guessed Skyler. *A female Nathan!*

Nathan gazed upward, as if pondering issues of global importance. Finally, he spoke: "As a bonus, I'll add Ninja Bloodbath II."

Baseball Cap Guy stood up. "Done."

There was a collective sigh of relief. Nathan and Baseball Cap Guy shook hands, ending with linked pinkie fingers. Everyone starting talking and passing around comic books. After a few minutes, Skyler and Julia snaked over to Nathan.

"Hey." Skyler's tone was friendly. "You said to meet here."

All conversation stopped abruptly.

Chapter Six

Everyone was staring at Skyler and Julia.

Skyler felt her cheeks get warm, remembering how she had stuck out at the Mathletes meeting. She wondered what his friends were thinking. Did they take her for an airhead because of her pink earmuffs and fur-trimmed high-heeled boots? They probably didn't know any Fashion Club members, just like she didn't know any Mathletes.

Oh, well.

"We've got, uh, something to do." Nathan coughed. "Anyone headed toward the mall?" A few kids shrugged and a ragged army started down the street: Surgical Scrubs Guy, Jasper the Martian, Batman girl, Nathan, Skyler, and Julia. Was this a group shopping trip? Skyler's heart sank.

But Nathan's friends peeled off one by one. "Afternoon Smackdown," explained Jasper. "Allergy shots," said someone else. The olive-skinned girl had to finish her diorama of Ancient Rome. At last, it was just Skyler, Julia, and Nathan.

Finally.

Nathan turned to Skyler excitedly. "Did you get us the gig?"

"Well — no," said Skyler, shaking her head. "The Valentine's Day Dance was booked. But guess what? You're playing the Student Health Carnival in April!" She tried to sound enthusiastic.

"Not until April?" Nathan's face fell. "That's suboptimal."

Skyler looked at Julia, and back at him. "Sorry," she said. "It was the best I could do, and to be honest, it wasn't easy to pull off."

"But you said —" Nathan kicked a stone on the ground. "You'll keep looking for other gigs, right?"

"Definitely. First we've got to update your look, though," said Skyler. "If you're serious about the band, you have to look cool." Julia looked worried, as if she might slip and use the word *makeover*.

Nathan winced. "Update it how?"

"New glasses," Julia said, too quickly.

"What's wrong with these?" he asked, adjusting his science safety goggles.

Skyler shrugged. "Nothing, if you're walking through plutonium."

They strolled through the atrium at Longbrook Court, the town's upscale mall. A tinny waterfall cascaded over a shiny black modern sculpture. Walking into The Eyes Have It, they were greeted by a long-haired man in a bowling shirt and tiny round blue glasses.

"I'm Stefan." The salesman smiled. "We have some very bold, exciting frames this season."

Nathan looked worried.

"These are nice," Stefan went on, holding up a red metallic pair, "if you want a retro-classic look."

Nathan frowned, but pulled off his safety goggles, giving Skyler got a better view of his face. He had brown eyes, and a crooked, shy smile. Nathan picked out a pair of wire-rimmed specs.

"Too Harry Potter," pronounced Julia.

Stefan handed Nathan a pair of oversize wood-and-steel aviators. "Designer," he said. "*Very* big this season."

"Literally." Nathan agreed, placing them in the reject pile.

Pretty soon, Nathan had a pile of discarded glasses on the counter. As Skyler squinted at the display case, she tried to think creatively.

41

Take Nathan's style and turn it up a notch: geek chic.

"Try these." Skyler handed Nathan some funky, rectangular frames. "They say, 'I'm cool, but I know what a parallelogram is.'"

Nathan laughed, and looked at Skyler, as if noticing something about her for the first time. Skyler felt pleased, and a little shy — the outing was turning out better than she'd hoped. Julia and Stefan came over and nodded in approval when Nathan put on the cool, brown frames. Skyler rearranged his bangs, making a note to visit a hair salon ASAP.

Nathan looked — actually — not too bad.

"My mom gave me her credit card," Nathan said. "She's been on me to get new clothes and stuff."

Skyler smiled. Maybe this would be easier than she thought.

The next stop was The Factory, a store that looked like the inside of a warehouse, with metal beams, graffitied walls, and pounding rap music. Julia and Skyler flipped through racks of clothes while Nathan watched a skateboarder on the video screen above them. The two girls argued about what Nathan's look should be.

"Old-school hip-hop," said Julia.

"Edgy prepster," disagreed Skyler. "Let me show you."

A few minutes later, she set a bundle of clothes in front of Nathan. "Oversize suit jacket," she said. "Graphic tee with a striped Oxford shirt." Skyler tossed him a porkpie hat. She added baggy chinos, a two-tone scarf, and green canvas messenger bag.

It was fun — like dressing a doll.

"I don't really like . . ." Nathan began, but Skyler pressed him into a dressing room.

When he came out, the striped shirt was buttoned all the way up, his slight frame overwhelmed by the jacket's massive shoulders. The two-tone scarf, meant to be a fun accent, looked like it was strangling him. The chinos were too long, so Nathan had rolled up the cuffs. The messenger bag dangled around his neck like a lifejacket. He looked utterly miserable.

"I'm choking," said Nathan.

"You just need a few adjustments," Skyler said, and quickly loosened the scarf.

Skyler showed Julia his shirt. "What do you think?" she asked. "It comes in Pebble, Ash, and Driftwood."

"It's okay, but look what I found," Julia said,

and pulled a hoodie, spray painted tee, and suede sneakers out of her shopping crate. "One hundred percent Destroyed Denim." She held up a pair of shredded jeans.

Nathan looked at the hoodie, which was stamped with giant numbers. "This isn't really my —"

"Sure it is," Julia interrupted with a wave her hand.

"Finding what you need?" A bored sales guy with a shaved head appeared out of nowhere. His T-shirt looked like it had been ripped halfway off his body. "Let me know if I can help," he said, staring at a rap video on-screen above them.

Nathan nodded, unable to move much in his over-layered outfit. He picked up a pair of painter's jeans on a table. "These are semi-acceptable," he grumbled. Skyler glanced at them quickly.

"No, I don't think so. Try these." She pushed him back into the dressing room, tossing him a pair of cords. Skyler and Julia resumed arguing over looks for Nathan.

"Beachy boho!"

"Egghead cool!"

The argument was getting heated, when Nathan's voice from the dressing room interrupted them.

"Um, guys?" he shouted through the door. "Did anyone see my garter snake?"

The shaved-head sales guy looked alarmed. Skyler looked at Julia, who almost dropped the quilted bomber jacket she was holding.

"I always say" — Nathan's voice was loud — "you can't appreciate denim if you're wearing underwear."

People started staring in their direction. Two teenage girls were giggling. A mother stopped wheeling her stroller. A guy in a soccer shirt elbowed his friend.

"Skyler," Nathan shouted again. "You know I vomit when I'm claustrophic!"

What in the world was Nathan up to?

The sales guy marched up to the door of the dressing room, while Skyler and Julia looked on, horrified. "Nathan!" Skyler called. "Come out of there!"

Nathan reappeared a moment later wearing his own clothes. The sales guy sighed and walked away.

"Are you *crazy*?" Skyler hissed.

Nathan seized a nearby mannequin. Dragging it over to the three-way mirror, he gripped it from behind, as if taking a hostage. In his other hand, he clenched a Converse All Star like a hand grenade.

"Stand back," he warned. "Or the sweater vest gets it."

"Nathan." Skyler pulled him aside, and he dragged over the mannequin. "Shhhh!"

"We need ground rules." Nathan planted the mannequin next to him. "No T-shirts with French words. No logos. Nothing Pre-Ripped, Vintage Wrecked, or Classic Shredded. I won't wear pants below my underwear, and gym shoes should . . . never . . . be . . . PLAID!" He knocked over the mannequin, which sent a rack of polka-dot briefs tumbling.

Well — who knew?

Nathan had opinions, likes and dislikes. They had to pay more attention to him, Skyler realized. The makeover stuff had been too much all at once. She certainly didn't want another scene! What a strange guy.

"I can live with that," Skyler said.

She helped collect the scattered briefs, and dragged the mannequin back to his home under the surfboard.

Leaving The Factory was a huge relief.

Skyler and Julia hit the juice bar for banana-mango smoothies, while Nathan stopped at Roderick's Dungeon. They had a few minutes alone, and couldn't wait to discuss his outburst at the store. They sank into chairs at the food court.

"The thing he said about the garter snake —"

"Not wearing underwear —"

"Vomiting when he's —"

Skyler shook her head, remembering the surprise of it. Then she burst out laughing.

"Skyler!" Julia's voice was shocked. "He just embarrassed us in front of half the mall!"

Now Skyler couldn't stop. "You have to admit, it was . . ." Skyler gasped for breath. "Pretty funny. Holding that mannequin hostage . . ."

Julia folded her arms.

"'Stand back, or the sweater vest gets it'!" Skyler continued. Finally, Julia cracked a tiny smile.

"Now *that* was psycho," Julia admitted.

Skyler's view was suddenly blocked by a blue-and-gold football jersey. Square letters spelled out WOLVERINES. Skyler looked up, startled.

"What it is," said Kyle Townshend.

Skyler sat up straighter. Her crush was standing in front of her, tossing waffle fries into his mouth. Looking at Kyle's broad shoulders, blond curls, and lazy smile, it was easy to see why he was at the top of most hottie lists. Skyler's heart began to pound.

A few steps behind him were other "cool" table kids: Sienna and Madison, holding pink-and-black shopping bags in one hand and cell phones in the other. *Oh no* — Nathan was going to be here any minute! It was much too soon to trot him out in public, before she'd had a chance to work on him.

"What'd you get?" Madison eyed Skyler's bag from The Factory.

"Baby tee," said Skyler without enthusiasm.

Just then, Nathan showed up in his futuristic jacket and safety goggles, carrying a paper bag with gothic lettering. "I forgot where we were supposed to meet." Nathan held up his cell. "Didn't know your digits."

Kyle looked at Nathan up and down and burst out laughing. "You guys are *friends*?" he asked, looking from Nathan to Skyler.

Hmmm — interesting test. If she was really serious about helping him, she had to go out on a limb. Here was her chance to give him a boost.

"Sure." Skyler gulped.

Nathan's eyes grew wider, taking this in. "Sorry for going postal on you before," he said, looking at Skyler and Julia. "Those security alarm tags emit mutant death rays."

Kyle laughed again, sizing up Nathan. "Where'd

you find this guy?" he snorted, sinking a paper cup into the trash with a hook shot.

Madison turned icily to Nathan. "Have we met?"

"Dunno," Nathan said. He had started to play a game on his cell phone.

"I'm Madison."

Nathan didn't respond.

"He's Nathan," said Skyler.

"Greetings and salutations," he finally replied without looking up.

"What are you doing here?" asked Sienna.

"Nathan needed clothes." Julia held up a shopping bag.

"Where'd you shop?" Madison looked at the row of pens in Nathan's shirt pocket. "Office Depot?"

Madison and Sienna bumped fists, and Kyle barked with laughter. Nathan gave a half smile. *He doesn't realize they're laughing at him*, thought Skyler miserably. She gave Julia a helpless look. They had to get him out of there.

"C'mon, Nathan." Skyler stood up. "Let's go."

"Chill," Kyle said, waving his hand at Skyler, and she reluctantly sat down. "What'd you buy?" He nodded at Nathan's bag from Roderick's Dungeon. "You like sci-fi?"

"SF." Nathan sniffed. "Nobody says sci-fi."

49

"Ex-cu-u-u-u-u-se *me*." Kyle snorted again. "Killer jacket, bro." He pointed to Nathan's silver wings. "You look like *The Thing from Outer Space*."

That was it. Skyler stood up again, pulling Nathan by the sleeve. Julia grabbed her anime bag and the three of them walked away. Before they left the food court, Nathan turned back and called to Kyle.

"The '56 original or '98 remake?"

Madison, Kyle, and Sienna looked at each other, puzzled.

Skyler sighed. Geek Rescue was done for the day.

Chapter Seven

"You here to play DragonSpawn?" The voice behind the closed door wasn't Nathan's.

"What?" Skyler asked.

It was two days after their mall excursion, and Skyler and Nathan were supposed to get together. Skyler checked the address he'd given her: 1015 Juniper Terrace. It was a pleasant ranch-style house with a log fence and a ceramic leprechaun on the lawn.

"I came to see Nathan," said Skyler.

"Oh," said the voice.

A few moments passed. "Well, can you go get him?" Skyler was annoyed. What was this guy's *problem*?

Finally, the door opened, and a head with long, straw-colored hair peeked out. It was Jasper Resnick, who had been at the outdoor comics-trading session. She remembered his wireless radio and Martian-like antennae.

Jasper looked at her ski-bunny jacket and frowned.

Nathan came up behind Jasper. "Let her in," he ordered. "She's a friendly unit." Leading Skyler inside, he motioned toward Jasper. "He's here hacking into the school computer."

"But I thought —" Skyler clutched her backpack.

"S'okay, he's in the basement." Nathan patted Jasper's back as he disappeared down a wood paneled staircase. "To the Batcave," said Nathan, and Skyler followed him down the hall. He pushed a door open.

"Wow." She looked around.

Every possible inch of wall space was crammed with miniature action figures, some in plastic boxes. A computer sat on a desk littered with X-ray glasses of blue and red cellophane. A glow-in-the-dark constellation map covered the ceiling. A fake bloody ax hung from the wall.

"Circus peanut?" He offered a bag of orange candy.

"No thanks." She was busy taking in the scene around her. Looking closer, Skyler could see shelves stuffed with books: *The Hobbit. Treasure Island.* A graphic story collection called *Pink Lipstick.*

"Pink Lipstick?" She raised her eyebrows at him.

"It's for girls," Nathan admitted, his ears reddening. "But the art is great."

Refreshing, thought Skyler. Kyle Townshend wouldn't be caught dead with a book like that. She scanned a bulletin board with strange postcards: World's Largest Twine Ball. The Shuffleboard Hall of Fame. The Soup Tureen Museum.

"I collect postcards from boring places. This summer I'm going to see the World's Largest Gas Station."

"No way," said Skyler. The guy *was* weird.

"Way."

As she collapsed onto an inflatable chair, she heard a crunch beneath her. She reached below and removed a box of bursting with tiny bones.

"Careful!" Nathan sounded annoyed. "That's an alligator skeleton."

Yuck! She handed the box to Nathan and brushed the bottom of her pencil skirt, hoping nothing had stuck.

"Where did you get it?" Skyler asked, trying to pretend she wasn't grossed out.

"Reptile farm." Nathan shook the box.

Where else?

"They have a monthly feeding where they release fifty rats into a room with twenty snakes."

"Should we start?" Skyler asked, ready to change the subject.

Nathan sat on his bed, sweeping a box of action figures out of the way. "Shoot."

"I've made a list of words you should start working into conversations." Skyler tore a sheet of paper out of a pink fur notebook and handed it to him.

Nathan sat up and read the list. "This class reeks. That car is dope. This party is raging. I am down with that." He said each phrase carefully, as if trying to memorize it.

"Um." She tossed back her hair. "You don't have to, like, *enunciate*."

"That shirt is classic," he continued reading. "The homework is harsh. Can you do me a solid? I got it going on."

Coming from him, the words didn't sound right. "Okay, we'll try something else." Skyler took back the list. "We'll have a conversation, and I'll tell you how to say stuff in a better way." Skyler scanned her mind for topics. "How are the Mathletes doing this year?"

Nathan leaned forward eagerly. "Well, we cratered at regionals, which was suboptimal —"

"You mean you tanked, which was bad," she corrected.

"Roger that," he said. "But we dialogued with some new life-forms —"

"Kicked it with other kids?" Skyler guessed.

". . . and they invited us to a primo quest . . ."

"Ragin' party." She was almost enjoying this.

"Except: negative females."

"No girls." Skyler nodded sympathetically.
Not surprising!

"Hey, you know . . ." Skyler looked at Nathan. "I like the way you talk. You have this cool way of putting words together. No one ever called me a 'friendly unit' before."

Nathan nodded. "But?"

"But right now you need to talk like everyone else." Skyler sat back in the chair. "Otherwise people will think you're weird." Here she was, complimenting Nathan's originality — then telling him to stifle it. But talking about a "primo quest" wouldn't fly at the cool table.

"No techie-speak," Skyler said firmly. "No words that end in '-oid.' No sentences starting with 'Methinks.'"

Nathan looked deflated. She felt a pang, but she couldn't let him get eaten alive by people like Madison.

"I think we did really well today!" Skyler stood up.

The bedroom door flew open, and Jasper walked in, chuckling. "You'd think the school administration would change their password once in a while." He wiped his neck with a napkin. "Well, mission accomplished: Broccoli florets are no longer on the lunch menu."

Nathan leaped up to give him their funny handshake.

"Jasper, Nathan and I were just having a chat." Skyler hoped he would take the hint.

"Offline?" He looked confused.

Skyler glanced at her watch, which had her favorite monkey logo on it. "Gee — look at the time," she said, getting to her feet. "I've got to run." She wondered what reason Nathan had given Jasper for her visit. "Thanks for the math tutoring," Skyler said to Nathan, pleased to think of an alibi.

"Anytime." Nathan didn't miss a beat. "Call if you have more trouble with infinitesimals. . . ."

"Definitely." Skyler winked.

As she pulled on her ski jacket, she heard Jasper ask Nathan, "You're teaching her *advanced calculus*?"

Skyler waved good-bye.

Jasper looked up, and Skyler could see him reevaluating her. It was fun to have a secret.

Chapter Eight

A few days later, Skyler and Julia were walking down the hall. Julia was describing her ensemble, a stylish-looking hazmat suit. "Industrial glam," she said. Her outfits often required an explanation.

"The metallic belt gives it sparkle," Julia added. "See —"

She was interrupted by a burst of noise at the end of the hall. Cries of "Ooh" and "Gimme that!" came from the crowd gathered in front of them. Skyler and Julia looked at each other, puzzled. It was three fifteen, only seconds after school had let out. What was going on?

The crowd seemed to be clustered around the statue of Maynard Siebert, the school's founder. Normally, Mr. Siebert was dignified and serious, glancing upward and thinking Great Thoughts. Today, he was stuffed into a slinky camisole with a string of pearls around his neck.

Skyler and Julia stared for a moment.

"Flirty is a good look for him," Julia decided.

His outfit had drawn a crowd. In front of the statue, Sienna and Madison were handing out PASSION FOR FASHION tank tops and leather bracelets from a cardboard box.

"Wrist cuff?" Madison offered. "Tank top?"

As usual, Sienna played the loyal sidekick. "Madison designed them," she gushed.

Skyler picked up a shirt, fingering the raised pink cursive lettering. Was this about Madison's bid to become Fashion Club prez? The election was a month and a half away — and campaigning outside the club was against the rules. Once again, Skyler felt outdone.

"Can you imagine what this *cost*?" whispered Julia.

Skyler turned to Madison. "Nice shirts," she shouted over the noise. "Why are you doing this?"

Madison smiled sweetly. "No reason."

Right.

"Party's over, ladies," said a deep voice behind them. Mr. Fisher, the school security guard, pointed to the statue. "Lose the undershirt. That's an order." The tall, bald man looked angry. "And take away the box. You can't do this on school property."

"It's not an undershirt," explained Sienna. "It's a *cami*."

"I don't care if it's your great-grandmother's drawers," Fisher said. "I want it OFF."

His words sent Madison scurrying to close up the box, while Sienna de-camisoled Maynard. A lacy strap got caught on his marble spectacles, and she had to squeeze it over his unsmiling face.

"Break it up now," said Mr. Fisher, like he was shooing away pigeons. "You heard me!" Girls scattered, heading toward the main exit.

Skyler and Julia followed the flow. "What is Madison up to?" asked Skyler suspiciously. "The election isn't for weeks."

"She's deeply concerned for the accessory-deprived." Julia's voice was sarcastic. "She's clever. It's not official campaigning, but it's good publicity. Everyone knows what going on."

Skyler swallowed. If Madison was pulling out all the stops to become Fashion Club president, it was time for Skyler to step up her efforts with Nathan. Where was he, anyway? They were supposed to meet after school.

A figure appeared at the end of the hall. "Skyler!"

She recognized Nathan's voice, and waved. Even from a distance, she could see his jacket was an unflattering shade of beige. She felt a wave of despair. Why wasn't he wearing any of his cute new clothes?

"Are you guys meeting today?" asked Julia.

"I almost forgot," Skyler said. "I snagged the Multipurpose Room so I could teach Nathan slang. I said it was for 'important Fashion Club business.'"

"Go," Julia urged. "I'm off to draw on my new high-tops." She pointed at her new whiter-than-white sneakers. "Don't these just beg for purple Magic Marker?" She waved at both of them, and slipped out of the double doors.

Skyler leaned against a locker, waiting for Nathan to cut across the black-and-tan floor. Something about the way he walked announced his nerdiness from a distance. What was it?

"Nathan." Skyler held up her hand like a crossing guard. "Walk across the hall again."

Nathan scowled, but retraced his steps. Skyler made note of his jerky movements and hunched shoulders. He seemed to twitch around nervously, instead of just walking.

"Okay, now." Skyler observed him like a scientist. "Over to the trophy case."

"Why?" Nathan grumbled, crisscrossing the hall with loud, clomping steps, deliberately exaggerating. Two girls in warm-up suits walked by, bouncing a soccer ball. One of the girls giggled at Nathan and nudged her friend.

"Let's, uh, get some privacy," said Skyler. She walked over to the Multipurpose Room and opened the door, leading Nathan inside. They sat down on folding chairs, next to a metal table. The room's sleek carpet, fluorescent lights, and blackboard made their "lesson" seem a bit more serious.

"Walk again, but this time — like a jock," Skyler said. "Think Kyle Townshend." Just saying his name gave her a little thrill.

Nathan grunted. He stood up straighter and took a few steps.

Too tentative, Skyler thought. Kyle would act like he owned the place. "Be confident. I'll show you," she said.

Skyler stood up, trying to channel Kyle into every fiber of her being. Even though she had a crush on him, she had to admit Kyle was a little overconfident. What would it feel like to think you were God's gift to seventh grade girls? Making her movements big, Skyler strutted across the carpet like a burly, self-assured jock.

"Du-u-u-de," she drawled. "She wants me ba-a-a-a-a-d."

Imitating Kyle wasn't that hard.

Nathan gave her a dubious look. He walked across the room, swaying his shoulders. "Du-u-u-de." He flexed his arms, and kicked the coffee table. "Isn't he kind of obnoxious?"

Yes, but awfully cute. "He's okay," Skyler said, resting on a chair. "Stand tall this time and relax."

Nathan shuffled over to the window and folded his arms.

"So," said Nathan, "you want me to act like a jerk."

"Kyle's a little . . ." Skyler shrugged. "Full of himself. But he's insanely popular. Now do it again — and swagger. Like you don't care about anyone but yourself."

Nathan tried. His swagger looked more like a waddle.

"Are you saying that to be cool I have to be a jerk?" Nathan stopped in mid-waddle.

This discussion was taking a strange turn. "No, I —" She thought about the guys who were popular. "Well, I don't know. Maybe a little bit." It was true that girls often went for guys who had an edge — and then complained about how mean they were. It was kind of a contradiction.

Maybe the indifferent ones were more of a challenge.

"Stick your chest out." Skyler threw back her shoulders. "Show some attitude." He imitated her again, but his neck seemed to shrink into his shoulders. He looked at Skyler hopefully, but she shook her head.

Doggedly, he did the walk again.

And again.

And again.

And again.

Skyler could see how hard he was trying. But his walk was too purposeful, too earnest. It looked nerdy, somehow. If she could be just get him to be less eager.

"Make it more 'I don't care,'" she said. "Like: So what if I've seen *Star Wars* fifteen times? That's just how I roll."

Nathan padded back and forth, practicing. Skyler turned around and looked out the window. It was starting to get dark, and she could hear the whine of the wind outside. A few snowflakes were falling. She looked back at Nathan, who was still crisscrossing the room.

Something was slightly different.

"Hey." Skyler moved to a folding chair. "Do that again." Nathan tensed up his shoulders, then stopped himself. He strode across the room with deliberate slowness.

Maybe. Almost.

"Floppier arms," Skyler said in a low voice. Something was happening here; she didn't want to mess it up. Nathan moved across the carpet with a loose-limbed stroll that looked much less nerdy. In fact, it was kind of relaxed and cool.

"Nathan." Skyler jumped up. "You're getting it!"

He did another lap over to the dry-erase blackboard.

"That's it!" she shouted. "Keep going!"

He did the stroll again. Spinning around, he threw a candy wrapper into the green metal wastebasket.

"And he sinks it with a hook shot." Nathan mimicked a sports announcer. Looking pleased with himself, he lifted his chin. "Now will you help the band get gigs?"

"For sure," said Skyler. As soon as she got him up to speed, she thought. "We still have a lot to do," she reminded him. "But we've made a great start."

She made him walk again. He was standing up straighter, owning his turf. She didn't know who

65

she was more impressed with — Nathan for doing it, or herself for teaching him! Skyler leaped up to high-five him, and he stopped her.

"Secret handshake," Nathan said, balling her hand into a fist. "First you stack fists, then lick your pinkie finger. Like this." Nathan took her hand and demonstrated.

It was fun to have him teach *her* something.

Skyler's fist joined Nathan's, and she licked her pinkie finger. "Now turn around," he said. "And touch my finger behind your back." Not easy to do in a fitted wool blazer with fake prep-school crest.

"WHOA!" a girl's voice sputtered behind them. "Uh, um . . . excuse me!"

Skyler and Nathan broke apart and saw Hunter Waxman-Orloff standing at the open door. Being caught in a tangle with Nathan was embarrassing. Skyler felt her cheeks get hot.

"What in the . . . ?" Hunter looked around. "I thought *Fashion Club* was using this room."

"Fashion Club? Oh, right." Skyler had to think quickly. "We, uh —"

Nathan stepped forward. "Skyler and I were talking . . ." He paused. "About opening up the club to guys."

Skyler's jaw dropped. "Guys?" she repeated dumbly.

Then she realized: Nathan was covering for her.

"Why do girls get to have all the fun?" he said. "I'd like to be in a clothing meet —"

"Fashion show," Skyler corrected.

"Sweater contest —"

"Coat drive," interrupted Skyler.

Hunter's eyes slid down Nathan's outfit, from the "Mazes & Minotaurs" hat to the green polyester sweater with a loud snowflake pattern. The rubbery-looking knit was bunched up, revealing a slice of *Star Trek* T-shirt. Too-short brown pants, white socks, and black loafers were an extra bonus.

"What can I say?" Nathan asked. "Fashion is my life."

"Uh — er, that's nice." Hunter coughed. "Just be out by four thirty. We're having a Family Fun Friday." She shut the door abruptly.

Skyler and Nathan sank into chairs and dissolved into laughter. It was fun to see Hunter squirm.

"Thanks for the backup," said Skyler. "And speaking of outfits . . . ?" She looked at his sweater meaningfully.

"I got tired of my new clothes." He looked down at his outfit. "How bad is it?"

It was so terrible that — for a split second — Skyler wondered if it was actually cool. Some ugly clothing was so out, it was in. She leaned over to examine a flammable-looking sweater sleeve. No, she decided.

This was just *out.*

"Snowflake sweaters are a fashion crime," Skyler informed him.

"Give me a break." Nathan sounded irritated as he pulled it off. Stuffing it in his backpack, he became very absorbed in rearranging the pockets. "So, tomorrow night," he said casually, not meeting her eyes. "Want to watch *Revolt of the Astro-Zombies*?"

Skyler stared at him.

"Solar-powered zombies take over the government." He lifted the backpack onto his shoulder. "Classic."

"I, uh . . ." Skyler stammered. Getting together . . . watching a movie . . . about *zombies*? Was he out of his mind?

"I know, you already saw it," Nathan deadpanned. "We'll have to go with *Kung Fu Martian Bloodbath*."

"Uh . . ." Skyler's stomach started to flutter. "It's not like we're . . ."

Friends, she almost said. They had a project to do, but she didn't want to give the impression that —

"It's just for two hours and seven minutes," he said. "Unless you have to go to a benefit to cure hat-head, or something." He folded his arms and waited.

She laughed. It could be a teaching op, she supposed. But — on a Saturday night?

No way!

And yet, through her panic, Skyler felt a tiny stab of curiosity. What would it be like to hang with Nathan?

Hmmm.

"Well, uh, I'm not —" Skyler sputtered. "Maybe." She could just imagine telling Julia what she was doing Saturday night. Are you off your *onion*? she'd say.

Nathan was still waiting.

"I, um —" Skyler's mind was a blank.

Nathan tapped his feet.

"Okay." Despite her grudging answer, she was already wondering what to wear.

Chapter Nine

"Look." Nathan faked a double take. "It lives!"

On screen, Frankenstein's monster was rampaging through a cemetery. When Nathan found out Skyler had never seen a horror movie, he said they had to start with basics. Sprawled out on the couch in Nathan's den, they took turns reaching into a box of gourmet jelly beans. The room was comfortable, with wood paneling, shag carpeting, and an old steamer trunk for a coffee table.

Nathan had turned the lights off for extra spookiness.

Skyler pulled farther away from Nathan on the couch. She didn't want it to seem like a date or anything. Hopefully, the black leggings and over-size T-shirt she had paired with a thin belt screamed "just friends." Nathan was in his new striped button-down, after Skyler made him change out of a vomit-orange polyester shirt.

The monster wore moldy rags.

"Ew!" Skyler made a face. "Talk about risky fashion choices."

"What's he *supposed* to wear?" Nathan shrugged.

Skyler squinted at the screen. "A scarf," she decided. "To hide his neck bolts." Her makeover brain never stopped working.

Nathan popped a blue bean into his mouth. "Grapefruit."

Meanwhile, the mad doctor was sewing together body parts to create a monster bride. "It's so *fake*, it's hilarious," Skyler said. She couldn't take her eyes off the screen. Holding her fist above her mouth, she dribbled gray beans into it. The taste was familiar, but something she couldn't identify. Kiwi? Olives?

"I know," said Nathan happily. "See how low budget it is?"

"This makes the school safety video look like great acting." Skyler was getting into the spirit of it. The worse the movie was, the better. "Have some buttered popcorn." She dropped a yellow bean in front of him.

"The next part is genius." Nathan leaned forward. "He goes ballistic and blows up the castle." He spat some orange beans into a napkin. "Ix-nay on the carrot."

Skyler moved away, grossed out. "I feel sorry for his bride. All the guys she meets are creeps."

As she reached for candy, her eyes clung to the screen. The story was strangely absorbing. The poor doctor kept trying to build the perfect monster — but his experiments always ended in disaster.

"Did I tell you Jasper and I are making our own horror pic?" Nathan pulled a notebook off the floor. "*Revenge of the Mutant Hall Monitor.* We even got real fake blood."

He showed her a piece of paper with panels of hand-drawn scenes: a bloody hall pass, a face, a face very close up, an eye, an eyeball. "Here's the storyboard," he explained. "Shows every scene in the movie."

Skyler looked at Nathan's sketches. The pictures, drawn in careful Magic Marker, told the story of a robot roaming the halls, recruiting students for an alien race. That Nathan! The guy had so many interests, most of them totally weird, but he really went after them. He didn't just go to the cineplex; he made movies.

About mutant hall monitors, she reminded herself.

As he turned the page, a neon-green piece of paper fell out of the notebook. She swiped it off the floor. "Winter Comic Convention," she read. "What's this?"

"I go every year." He muted *Frankenstein*. "They hold it at the Longwood Inn. Kind of a freak show, but there's good stuff. Last year I met the guy who draws Doktor BrainBend."

Freak show? If *Nathan* said that, she could only imagine.

"There are signings by authors and artists, and people show up in insane costumes. Sometimes you can't even tell if it's a man or woman. Personally? I look at the Adam's apple."

"Wait a minute." Skyler looked at the flyer again. "It's the same day as the Valentine's Day Dance."

"Interesting factoid." He leaned over to look at the flyer. "Who knows what I'll do?"

Skyler sat up straight. "You can't miss the dance! It's your big debut!"

"Maybe." Nathan tossed the remote like a juggler. "Probably."

"Definitely!" She'd make sure of *that*. She noticed a black instrument case in the corner. "Nathan," she said, "whose flute is that?"

Nathan turned on the light. "My mom plays in a jazz ensemble. Want to see it?" He opened the case and handed it to Skyler.

Ahhhhh.

Skyler ran her hands over the smooth metal, fingering the familiar keys and curves. Impulsively, she assembled it, fitting the different pieces together, feeling the satisfying grip when the metal tubes connected. She held it in front of her, enjoying its weight and coolness.

"I used to play." Skyler remembered hours spent in the cozy school music room, with its wood-polish smell and hissing radiator. Going there felt like an hour out of time, snatched away from the noise of her life. "I was really into it. My teacher even asked me to join this youth orchestra. . . ." Her voice trailed off.

"And . . . ?" Nathan prompted.

Skyler felt her face redden. "I took a pass. Too nerdy." Her friends had called it "The Dorkestra."

"What?" Nathan tilted his head.

"I — never mind." Skyler put the flute down. "Nerdy" wasn't the best choice of words, considering.

"You gave up something you liked to do because someone thought it wasn't cool?" His tone wasn't harsh, just curious. "Why do they get to decide what's cool?"

"I don't know." Skyler twisted her turquoise ring.

She remembered the high school football game she went to, where the bedraggled marching band played the theme from *Rocky*. It had been hard to picture herself in the baggy red-and-gold uniform.

They looked like they were having fun, though.

Had she made the wrong choice? Orchestras and marching bands *were* nerdy, right? And there was no point in endless practicing, if she wasn't going to —

"Just asking." Nathan's voice was soft.

They were both silent.

"I'm not the only one who cares about public opinion. You wanted to learn how to be cool — remember?" Skyler was suddenly annoyed. It bugged her to be accused of mindlessly following the crowd.

"Affirmative." Nathan picked up the flute. "But that's to achieve specific goals at school, like getting my band a gig. I'm gaming the system. Here, I make my own rules." He pressed it to his lips and played a high note, holding it for a long time.

In Skyler's world, it wasn't that simple.

"Want to play?" He wiped the mouthpiece with a tissue and handed it back to her. "I'll get out my drums."

It felt like a dare. She reached out to finger the instrument again, cupping the mouthpiece, and holding the flute against her cheek.

"Okay." She shrugged.

He went to the corner of the room, and pulled a sheet up to reveal a spiffy electric blue drum set. Skyler came over to admire it.

With a tattered copy of *America's Best Loved Music*, they limped through folk songs, some Beatles, and a spectacularly bad version of "Sounds of Silence." It felt good to play again, even if it made her a little wistful. Skyler got up to stretch, and saw that the movie was still running.

"Notice how I didn't suggest the theme from *Star Wars*?" Nathan waved a sheet of music. "Now, *that's* progress."

Skyler laughed and turned on the sound. She scooped up some red speckled beans, thinking they looked like eggs from an exotic bird. On screen, the monster was thrashing around as his creator looked on, powerless.

Chapter Ten

"SAVE THE LAME EXCUSES, people," said Ms. Fortunato, the gym teacher, on Monday morning. "I don't care if you have a sprained earlobe, Video Game Finger, or your gym suit's at the cleaners," she said. "Today, we're doing something different."

She motioned for the class to sit, and thirty girls noisily slumped to the floor. "We're starting a modern dance unit." Everyone groaned. "Your assignment is a group interpretive dance, possibly performed for spring assembly."

Skyler looked at Julia. This was *not* good news.

"I need ideas for dance themes," barked Fortunato. "Hands?"

Everyone looked blank.

The teacher coughed and shifted her clipboard to her other hip. She was a sturdy redhead whose body language suggested she'd prefer to be back in her office, inflating dodgeballs.

"Change of seasons, power of love, world peace, reach for the stars," Fortunato rattled off in a bored voice. "C'mon, people, use your noggins."

Becca Frost raised her hand. "Can we do something pro-vegetarian?" Becca wore black nail polish and once wrote "Meat is Murder" in cherry lip liner on the locker room mirror. Skyler and Julia looked at each other and groaned.

"All ideas welcome. Break up into groups and discuss it."

The gym floor was soon dotted with clusters of girls chattering, fighting, and hair-braiding. Skyler viewed this as a perfect opportunity for some Julia-time, since her friend had been away all weekend. "On Wednesday I'm taking Nathan to Hair and Now," Skyler told her. "I can't wait to see what Dixon does with him."

Julia leaned back on her elbows, kicking off her new high-tops, which she had decorated with purple and red markers. She wore fringed cotton socks, a yellow bandanna, and a band button. Leave it to Julia to accessorize a gym suit.

"Can he cut off that scraggly part in the back?" Julia's voice was hopeful.

"Yes," said Skyler, more excited than she meant to be. "I want to keep it messy — but in the right way. He looks better, wearing those button-down shirts we got him. Plus plain tees, and broken-in jeans. And he's not hunching over when he walks."

"HAN-son!" Fortunato gave Skyler a look reserved for people who throw the bat in softball. "*Dance* themes."

"On it." Skyler turned back to Julia. She wanted to tell Julia about Saturday night, but didn't know how to bring it up. "I've been — getting to know him more, I guess. He's pretty funny. We were watching this *Frankenstein* movie, and . . ."

Julia's eyes widened. "You watched a movie together?"

"This dumb horror flick." Skyler waved her hand. "But later that night —"

"Whoa, whoa, whoa." Julia bolted upright. "This was at *night*?"

Skyler knew she had dropped a bomb, but wasn't sure what to say. She tried downplaying it. "Yeah, Saturday. You were in Milwaukee —"

"SATURDAY night?" Julia's asked loudly. A few girls looked at her.

"Shhhh." Skyler put her finger over her mouth. "We were working on stuff!" But if Julia was so freaked out by the movie get-together, it was better not to give details. Skyler smiled, thinking about their crazy jam session.

"You gave him a Saturday night." Julia lowered her voice. *"Are you out of your mind?"*

"It was no big deal," said Skyler, getting nervous. She knew Julia would overreact to this.

"If you say so," Julia said finally. They sat in silence, listening to taunts, screams, and laughter all around them.

"Well." Julia kicked a pink gumwad. "What was it like?

"What was *what* like?" Skyler was guarded.

"It. Him. The evening."

Choose your words carefully, Skyler told herself.

"He's really interesting." Skyler felt her voice rise. "He reads graphic novels and makes horror movies, and collects postcards from boring places." Hmmm — maybe that last point didn't advance her argument. "He's not what you think."

"Huh. Okay." Julia nodded her head.

The evening had a strange effect on her, Skyler wanted to say. Her world felt bigger that night, doing things she had never done before —

watching a campy movie, playing a duet for fun. It was nice to talk to a boy who asked *her* questions, instead of just describing the awesome catch he made in the fourth quarter. She kept replaying their conversation in her head.

"He's got all these weird interests," said Skyler, "but underneath it all, he's a —"

"Mathlete," blurted Julia.

Skyler was confused. "Yes, but —"

"And you're in Fashion Club."

Did that mean they couldn't be *friends*?

"Skyler, do you like him? I mean, *like*-like him?" Julia leaned forward.

"Of course not!" Skyler sat up straight, shaking her head angrily. Like-like him? For God's sake!

Skyler felt ambushed by the question, since she considered Julia a fellow Nathan-ologist, someone who enjoyed puzzling him out. Didn't Julia understand that her interest in Nathan was almost, well, scientific? It was like they were studying an interesting species together.

Julia sat back, resting on her elbows. "Good. Whew." She sounded relieved. "I mean, I didn't think so, but . . ." Julia's voice turned gentle. "You're the first girl who's ever paid attention to him, probably. Just — be careful not to get his hopes up. That's all I'm saying."

81

Skyler sighed noisily.

Wasn't it Nathan who made the speech about "gaming the system"? They were using *each other*. True, Skyler had had the same fears Julia was expressing when Nathan invited her over — which is why she'd hesitated. But it had all worked out. "Nathan knows this is just business," Skyler said. "He's doing this to get his band —"

Someone walked between them. Skyler followed a pair of floral leggings up to the gymsuit, and saw that it was Madison. She and Jameeka and Sienna plunked down next to them. Hopefully, they hadn't heard her rant.

"What up, girlfriends," said Madison. "We're, like, not inspired."

Sienna's blond curls were pinned back and tied up in a chiffon scarf. "Do you guys have any ideas?" She tucked back a stray lock of hair. "'A Night to Remember'? 'Viva Las Vegas'? 'We Are the World'?"

"Dance themes. Not *prom* themes." Madison snorted.

"'Night of a Thousand Gym Suits'?" Julia offered.

"Ladies?" Fortunato barged up to them with a clipboard. "I'm ready for your ideas." Fortunato turned to a girl who was laughing loudly.

82

"CAFFERTY," she yelled. "Put a cork in it!" Then her gaze fell on Skyler.

"Any ideas, Hanson?"

Why *her*? What rotten luck.

"Um, maybe, uh, something about . . ." Skyler tried to muster up an idea. She looked around at clusters of brawling girls. "People."

So, *so* lame.

"People." Fortunato glared. "What about 'em?"

Skyler had to make something up — fast. Staring at her checkered slip-on sneakers, she saw a red line on the floor. "We're all dancing in a line, see," she said, hoping for an idea. "One girl falls out of line. And they keep on dancing without her." Skyler nudged Julia.

"Dancing without her," repeated Julia.

Big help.

"Then the girl . . ." Skyler's mind was blank. Think of something — *anything*! "Makes up her own dance. And it gets wilder and wilder."

Behind them, two girls taunted each other. "Shut up." "No — YOU shut up!"

"GOOD LISTENING BEHAVIOR!" Fortunato's voice was hoarse.

Skyler got an idea. "The group comes back," she said. "To bring her into line. But she *likes* doing her own thing."

"So?" Fortunato prompted.

"She won't come back." Skyler had a brainstorm. "And the group is mad. Then someone notices how much fun she's having, and *that* girl breaks away, too. Pretty soon, everyone's spinning off in their own direction."

Skyler looked around. Julia, Madison, and Sienna were all staring. How had she come up with *that*?

"People. Change. Done." Fortunato wrote on her clipboard. "Hanson, you be squad leader." Fortunato pointed at her and broke into a jog. "INDOOR VOICES, PEOPLE!" She blew her whistle and headed for the double doors.

"I'm impressed." Madison took Skyler's elbow as the crowd streamed out of the gym. "You sounded like you knew what you were talking about."

"Do we all wear the same costume?" Sienna sounded worried. "Leotards make my butt look big."

The roar of the crowd drowned out Skyler's answer, as a swarm of girls stormed the locker room. When they reached their gym lockers, Julia turned to Skyler. "Dancing in a line? Breaking away? Sheesh!"

"I had to say *some*thing." Skyler climbed out of her gym suit, uneasy about their earlier conversation. "Look, about Nathan — I *am* careful of his feelings. What's wrong with getting to know him?" Skyler tried for a brisk tone. "That way I can see where he needs help."

"Nothing's wrong with it." Julia squirmed into a vintage Rolling Stones tee. "Seriously. As long as you think about what to do with him when this is all over. You can't just use him for this project and then —" Julia squeezed into knickers. "Dump him."

Skyler felt a flash of irritation. She had more urgent worries, like finding a trial outing for Nathan. She wanted to test his skills with a new crowd, preferably from a different school. Passing him off as a cool guy somewhere else would be great practice for the Valentine's Day Dance.

"Julia." Skyler knew she sounded slightly obsessed. "How do you think Nathan would do at Velvet Stern's bat mitzvah?"

"Let me put it this way," said Julia slowly. "How would *you* do at the Westinghouse Science Fair?"

Score one for Julia. But Skyler had come this far, and she wasn't about to give up.

Chapter Eleven

"Ready to work?" asked Skyler, offering Nathan a bag of potato chips. They were perched on a bench in McKinley Park, watching skateboarders flip, twist, and grind. It was a warm day for January, and the skate park was packed. She had brought Nathan there to get used to cooler hangouts. But instead of watching the skateboarders, he kept turning around to look at the chess players.

"Pawn to b4," Nathan muttered, shaking his head. "It's *obvious*."

Skyler sighed and pulled out her pink fur notebook. Valentine's Day was three weeks away, and they had major work to do. In the background, they heard cries of "Wicked air, bro!" and "Sick finish!"

"Turn around." Skyler did a clothing check. Everything he wore was something she'd picked out at the mall: green North Face jacket, work shirt, long-sleeve crew tee. "I'm lovin' the outfit," she said. "Except for this."

She reached over to remove a hat with fleece earflaps, but he swatted her hand away. Skyler sighed and opened her notebook. "Today, let's work on conversation. Stuff like, what do you say to someone at the bat mitzvah?"

Nathan swiped a stick off the ground.

"Good topics are: TV shows, movies, who sucked on *American Idol*," Skyler barreled on. "The Bulls game, a piece of clothing you can only get in New York, soccer, what you bought at the mall, how the mini-quesadillas rock but the egg rolls are generic."

"I don't —" Nathan looked away.

"Some things can only be complained about." Skyler was enjoying herself. "Homework, assemblies, Locker Safety Week . . ." She smoothed the pink fur on her notebook. " 'Edutainment' videos, health class."

"So you mean I —" Nathan tried.

"Don't act too smart," she said. "Complain about math even if you know what a rhomboid is. And don't get too excited about anything.

Notice how cool kids act kind of bored? Like, 'big whoop.' "

Nathan drew on the ground with his stick, while Skyler raced on.

"Don't mention Mathletes, Book Buddies, or tech lab." She wrinkled her nose. "If anyone asks about future careers, say 'billionaire' or 'race car driver.' Okay hangouts are here, Starbucks, and the waterfall at the mall." She stopped to catch her breath. "You do any sports?"

Nathan thought a moment. "I rock at tetherball."

"Forget sports."

"I'm also a gifted —" Nathan began.

Skyler interrupted. "Playing video games, making movies, being in a band — all good. If someone sees you going to the Renaissance Faire, say you thought it was a monster truck rally."

Nathan broke the stick in half. "Could I please get a word in edgewise?"

Skyler looked at him, startled.

"This is all useful input, but —" He wedged his Nike between the slats of the bench. "Listen to yourself. 'Don't act too smart. Be more boring.' " He peered at the chess table. "Your friends sound like morons." Nathan scowled. "No offense."

Skyler felt stung. "You're the one who wanted to fit in!"

"Yeah, but —" He squinted into the sun. "I didn't realize I'd have to delete so many brain cells."

"You don't!" Skyler protested, while at the same time wondering if it was true. Was not broadcasting math chops the same as dumbing yourself down? At lunch, she stayed silent when certain complaint-worthy subjects came up, like jazz band, the Nature Center, or the free write portion of English class. She didn't admit that she found some jocks at school kind of boring.

Or certain Mathletes kind of interesting.

"Craigmore the Invincible!" Someone yelled behind them. "Surrender your jewels!"

They spun around, and saw a high-school-aged guy step off a Razor scooter. He had long hair, wire-rimmed glasses, and a T-shirt that read VARSITY PHYSICS. In his hand was a bag from the Apple store.

Nathan's face lit up. "My Dungeon Master. Milo, this is Skyler."

Milo half bowed to Skyler.

"I'd slay a thousand men to carry your backpack," he said conversationally.

Skyler rolled her eyes, but moved over on the bench. Milo sat down and cast a bored eye at the skateboarders, while Nathan stared at Milo.

"Excellent T-shirt," Nathan said.

"The clothes make the man," Milo looked down at himself. "What can I say?"

"New toy?" said Nathan, pointing to his Apple bag. Milo opened it, and Nathan peered inside.

"Wow," said Nathan. "I'm dying to get one."

"S'okay," sniffed Milo. "The actual formatted capacity isn't that impressive."

"Oh," said Nathan.

Milo looked at his watch and jumped up. "Must go. The orthodontist awaits." He bowed to Skyler, and drew Nathan into a private huddle. He wagged his finger, like an older brother offering serious advice.

"Remember," he said. "A girlfriend is no substitute for video games."

Nathan's cheeks turned red.

"We're not —" he started to protest, but Milo was already pulling away on his scooter. Nathan and Skyler looked at each other, and then looked away quickly.

"Hey!" Nathan shouted after him. "Want to see *The Eliminator*?"

"Waste of eyeballs," Milo shouted back.

Nathan sat down on the bench, following Milo with his eyes until he disappeared. Skyler was still trying to absorb the word "girlfriend." Unconsciously, she pulled farther away from him on the bench.

"Waste of eyeballs," repeated Nathan. "I've got to use that one."

It was interesting to see him so . . . dazzled. "Do you have a crush on him or something?" teased Skyler.

Nathan gave her a look.

"He's the coolest guy I know," Nathan continued. "People hang on his every word. His approval can make a quest or ruin it."

"Like Ashleigh Carr." Skyler thought about the school's queen bee. So Nathan had a guru, too. "If you hang on his every word . . ." Skyler smiled. "Doesn't that make you a mindless drone like the rest of us?"

"Yeah." Nathan smiled. "But at least *my* role model is freakishly smart."

Whatever.

"Let's have a practice convo!" Skyler sat up straight. "We're in the lunch line. Pretend we never met." She tucked her fur boots under her. "Fish sticks? Haven't had those in a while."

"Yup." Nathan nodded. "In food fights, they make excellent projectiles."

"Um," said Skyler. "Right. Any other topics?"

"So." Nathan jiggled his keys. "Did you know black widow spiders kill after mating?"

"What?" Skyler jumped up, dropping her notebook. "No. *No!* Never mention insects. *Ever.*"

"Spiders are arachnids." His voice was haughty. "Not insects." He closed his eyes like he was trying to focus. After a few moments, he turned to Skyler. "Did you watch *Heroes* last night?"

"Good topic!" Skyler clapped. Maybe this was finally working. "Now tone it down. Be more bored."

Nathan looked amused. Picking up another stick, he repeated the words in a robotic monotone.

"Fewer words," she said. "Like you're texting someone. U see *Heroes*? Like that."

Skyler put down her notebook. It was nice just sitting there with Nathan in the sunshine, hearing the sound of wheels grinding, people shouting, and bodies hitting the pavement. She closed her eyes and arched her neck, enjoying the heat on her forehead.

"Let's try again." Skyler tossed a chip at him. "You got Graber for history?"

"Yeah. I'm so . . ." Nathan spoke carefully. ". . . *Over* the Constitution."

Good, Skyler thought. "You going to the mall after school?"

"Maybe," he said. "Got to get new . . ."

Skyler waited.

" . . . Basketball shoes," he finished.

"Yes!"

Nathan continued. "Have you been —" he corrected himself. "U playing flute?"

Were they still pretending to be strangers? Skyler looked down at her yellow leather gloves. She felt a pang remembering how fun their jam session was. Why couldn't *that* be cool, instead of rating outfits in the lunchroom? "Naah. You reading any online comics?"

"No, just regular ones. Sometimes I like . . ." He paused. "Kickin' it old school."

"You're catching on! Fantastic!" Skyler nodded happily.

Just then, a skater took a dive and landed at their feet. A high school guy in a white helmet squirmed on his back, clutching his knees. His whole body was streaked with dirt.

"Sorry," the skater said as he sat up. "Was stoked for a manual but my tail dragged." He took a few swipes at dusting himself off, which only made him dirtier.

Skyler nudged Nathan. "Talk to him," she urged.

Nathan folded his arms defiantly. Then, after a second, he turned to the skater. "Hey, man," Nathan said, "doesn't that curfew totally reek?"

Skyler could have kissed him. But she settled for pouring the rest of the potato chips on his lap.

Chapter Twelve

Skyler rang the doorbell and prayed.

Please, please, let Nathan look cute today.

She had come by Nathan's house to take him to Velvet Stern's bat mitzvah party. Her father stayed in the car while Skyler waited for Nathan, shivering in the camel's hair jacket she had slung over her strapless ice-blue dress. Fidgeting with the pearl bracelet she'd borrowed from her mother, Skyler hoped Nathan had taken her grooming advice. Finally, the door opened.

She almost didn't recognize him.

Nathan stood before her in sharp khaki pants, a light blue shirt, and khaki jacket. His brown shoes were broken in just the right amount. His hair was appealingly mussed, and his new glasses only slightly lopsided. He darted into his closet to pull out his new North Face jacket and a battered dark green messenger bag.

"You look awesome!" Skyler said, and meant it.

He looked relieved. "Thank you, milady." Nathan bowed and made curlicues with his hand. He dropped his keys, then bent down to grab them off the floor. His eyes widened as he took in her fancy dress and French twist hairdo. She could tell he was nervous.

So was she.

Even though she had picked out most of his outfit, she felt unexpectedly stirred by the sight of him. He had such a nice, shy smile. She flicked a speck of imaginary dust off his shoulders, which looked bulkier under his jacket. Had they always been that way?

Skyler pulled out the pink-and-yellow invitation, printed on see-through paper and tied with raffia. Confetti spilled out of the envelope. Skyler knew Velvet from summer camp and they stayed in touch, even though they went to different schools. Skyler had met Velvet's friends a couple times before at parties in Velvet's rec room. They were supercool, the A-list from Northside, the middle school in a fancier suburb. She had found them a little intimidating.

Skyler remembered smart-looking girls talking about vacations in Aspen, and someone who owned her own horse. A cute guy bragged about having a rock-climbing wall at home. His name was Chace ("With a *c*," he had said in a bored voice). They were at the top of their school's food chain, like Skyler's group at Longbrook. True, she hadn't liked Velvet's friends much, but so what? Meeting them would be a good test for Nathan before hitting the cool crowd at their own school.

When they got outside, Nathan pointed at the silver minivan in the driveway.

"Parental units?"

"My dad," Skyler explained. "He doesn't bite."

They got in, and Skyler's father turned around to give Nathan a handshake. "Dave Hanson." He smiled approvingly. He was a big man with short gray-blond hair, wearing a ski jacket over sweats. "How do you two — ?"

"We know each other from school, Dad." Skyler shifted impatiently.

"Hello there." Nathan sounded strangled, as he leaned forward to shake. Skyler's father pumped his hand, and then turned up the radio for the score of the Bulls game.

Skyler turned to Nathan for a private convo. He stretched out his legs, and his knee brushed

97

Skyler's dress. They both pulled away from each other and he retreated to the far edge of the seat. Skyler gave him the 411 on Velvet. "I met her at summer camp. Did you ever go to . . . ?"

"Magic camp." Nathan picked something off the ceiling.

Of course.

Skyler explained that Velvet had been in her cabin, and she wasn't the sharpest tool in the makeup bag. But she was lively and fun, willing to share Skittles and make prank phone calls. All summer, Velvet had been obsessed with planning her bat mitzvah party, which took place the night after the religious ceremony. During free swim and archery, Skyler had listened to her agonize over choosing a party theme.

"Tropical Island Fantasy, Hollywood Nights, Tennis Anyone?, Harry Potter, Sixties Retro," Velvet would rattle off. "I can't decide. I could give away Hawaiian print boxers," she'd consider. "On the other hand, it's a once-in-a-lifetime chance to have a French fry toppings bar."

Sitting in the car with Nathan, that conversation seemed like a long time ago. Velvet had been psyched when Skyler asked if she could bring someone; the guest list was short on guys. "I hope he's brutally hot," Velvet had said.

Brutally hot was a tall order.

Before they picked Julia up, Skyler leaned over to give Nathan last-minute tips. "Hey," she whispered. "Make eye contact. Use a napkin. Don't talk to anyone for more than five minutes." She played with the sequins on her fancy purse. "Stroll around before you commit to a conversation. And leave while the party is still going on — it makes you look like you have better plans."

"Five minutes. Got it." He nodded.

Skyler was about to make another important point about mini–hot dogs, but Julia was climbing into the car. Ever since Julia had warned Skyler to be careful with Nathan, Skyler felt slightly self-conscious being around both of them at once. Her mind raced: Was she being too friendly to Nathan? Was she leading him on? Skyler tugged at her dress, so the blue satin didn't touch Nathan's pants.

As always, her best friend was funky in a black lace minidress and tiny denim jacket. Julia loved mixing super-fancy and informal clothes. Squeezing into the back seat, her eyes swept over Nathan and Skyler. "Who's the handsome guy?" she asked.

Nathan continued tracing a lightning bolt on the car window, but Skyler could see a faint smile on his face.

Her father pulled into the long driveway of a country club and waved good-bye. "Call when you need a ride," he said. They climbed out, and nearly collided with some cute guys tossing a mini-football. As Skyler watched the confident jocks stroll into the building, she felt her stomach drop.

Deep breath.

Opening the heavy glass door, she wondered what fantasy theme Velvet had decided on.

A woman with an enormous silver choker and a clipboard led them to a large party room. Velvet's name was written in giant pink foil letters on a sign on top of a raised platform. The entire room was filled with pink and yellow balloons and streamers, continuing the color theme of the invitation. Shopping bags hung from the ceiling, filled with colorful, shredded paper. Brooklyn Davis — another girl Skyler knew from summer camp — waved them over to her table.

"Aren't the decorations *off* the *hook*?" Brooklyn was a friendly, freckled redhead who always spoke overenthusiastically. "Only Velvet would come up with a shopping theme. I *love* it."

Skyler, Nathan, and Julia looked around the room. "It's supposed to be, like, a mall," Brooklyn explained, plucking a mini–egg roll off a tray offered by a waiter with a headset and a name tag that read THE GAP. She picked up a place card. "Every table is a different store. Isn't that awesome?"

When they found their place cards, Skyler and Nathan were seated at "J. Crew," and Julia was at "Abercrombie." Brooklyn was disappointed they weren't at her table. "I'm at 'Juicy Couture,'" she said. "Shoot."

"Nourishment?" Nathan looked around impatiently. The room was filling up with girls dressed in slit skirts, baby-doll dresses, and fancy beaded frocks. Guys came in, too, shedding jackets quickly to search for food or Foosball.

Brooklyn pointed to a bank of food stations where cooks stood flipping crêpes, rolling sushi, and folding burritos. "That's the food court." She gave a thumbs-up. "Fabulous." The four of them made a beeline for it, loading plates with maki rolls, mini-crêpes, fruit, and other goodies. The three girls looked at Nathan, whose head was thrown back as he stuffed celery stalks into his mouth. He looked like he was feeding lumber into a wood chipper.

"Slow down," Skyler whispered.

"Mmmmph," said Nathan.

"Guys!" Velvet waved to them from the middle of a crowd. Skyler could only see the top of her friend's curly blond head. Velvet motioned for them to join her, and Skyler dragged Nathan along.

As Skyler, Julia, Nathan, and Brooklyn approached Velvet's circle, they heard her voice before they saw her. " . . . simply could NOT decide," Velvet was saying. "So I looked deep down, and asked myself, 'What am I *really* interested in?' And then it hit me: shopping." A couple of skinny girls with sparkly hair ornaments were nodding energetically.

When Velvet saw Skyler and Julia, she enveloped them in a cloud of pink tulle and CK One.

"You look . . ." Skyler shook her head at Velvet. Her friend wore a silver lamé fitted strapless gown smothered in pink tulle, with a rhinestone tiara. She had glitter on her cheeks, and she teetered on silver open-toed high heels. Skyler glanced at Nathan to see his reaction to Velvet, but he was staring longingly at the food table. ". . . amazing," Skyler finished.

Velvet elbowed Skyler and eyed Nathan flirtatiously. "Introduce me," she said. Julia and Skyler exchanged glances. This was a good sign!

Meanwhile, Nathan was pressing buttons on his watch.

"Velvet, this is our friend, Nathan." Skyler steered him closer to the group. "Nathan, Velvet."

"Greetings and salutations." He nodded. Skyler winced; he was supposed to stick to "hey" or "yo." His eyes darted up to Velvet, then returned to his watch. They slid up to Velvet's face again, and this time, he stood up a little straighter. Skyler felt a quiver of annoyance.

Two guys broke into their conversation. A cute jock with thick, butter-yellow hair put a lazy arm around Velvet. "Hey, gorgeous." Skyler recognized his dark-haired buddy. "Chace," he said, introducing himself to Skyler and Julia. Apparently he didn't remember meeting them at Velvet's party last summer.

"With a *c*," Skyler added.

"Do we know each other?" Chace looked surprised. The blond guy smiled at her and Julia.

"Could be," Skyler said. It was fun to flirt. These guys reminded her of Kyle Townshend and other cute jocks at school.

The blond guy smiled. "I'm Grant." Chace pretend-punched him in the stomach.

Skyler turned around to prompt Nathan to introduce himself, but he was loudly crunching on

103

something. "Radishes," he said. The round red vegetable he held up was carved in the shape of a flower. "I feel a potassium low."

"Aren't those for decoration?" Skyler forced a smile.

Nathan shrugged. "They have enzymes that aid digestion."

Everyone stared. Skyler made up a new rule: Never say *enzyme* at a party. Or *digestion*. It was hard to keep anticipating his next blunder. Nathan crunched on, oblivious to other people's reaction. He pulled a glow stick out of his pocket, and twirled it like a light saber.

"Where'd you get that?" asked Chace.

"Over by Banana Republic," he said. It took Skyler a moment to realize he meant the table, not the store. "I took an extra one for Milo." When everyone looked at him blankly, he explained, "My Dungeon Master."

With great effort, Skyler managed to keep smiling. *This just gets better and better*, she thought.

Grant and Chace looked at each other as if to say, "Who *is* this guy?" Skyler wanted to kill Nathan. Didn't he remember *anything* she'd taught him?

Meanwhile, Velvet was still going on about her theme choice. ". . . personalized mini-basketballs." She tilted her head. "But I decided against X-Treme Sports —"

All conversation was suddenly cut off by a strange beeping sound. Grant and Chace backed away.

Beep-beep, beep-BEEP, BEEP-BEEP.

What was causing it? Skyler looked around, until she realized it was coming from . . .

Nathan!

He was frantically readjusting his calculator watch. "Stupid thing's in Helen Keller mode." People were staring.

"Turn that thing *off,*" Velvet hissed. "Hey, everyone." She tried to distract the crowd. "Remember to pick up your 'credit card,' and be sure to sign my Tiffany's box, and . . ."

The beeping stopped.

Finally.

Velvet, Skyler, and Julia all turned on Nathan. "What happened?" Velvet looked exasperated.

"Sorry." Nathan was apologetic. "Skyler said I shouldn't talk to anyone for more than five minutes, so I set my alarm."

Chace and Grant laughed and high-fived each

other. Skyler swallowed, and Velvet looked puzzled. Then she laughed, too.

"That's great." Velvet obviously decided to
take this as a joke. "What else did she say?"

Nathan shrugged. "Not to bring up She-Hulk
more than necessary." Velvet laughed — but
Skyler knew he was giving her a straight answer.
"Or Magic cards or Mathletes."

This was going downhill fast.

Before Velvet could respond, the big-necklaced
lady whisked her away. "Sorry, guys." Velvet blew
them a kiss. "Dancing's going to start, and I have
to make my entrance."

"Um, Nathan?" Skyler put her hand on his
elbow, and guided him to the side of the room.
"Could we, uh, chat for a minute?" As they veered
over, the sound of trumpets stopped them in their
tracks. On the pink foil stage, a cool-looking,
leather-jacketed young woman with a headset
appeared. "Ladies and Dawgs, please give it up for
the might-tay, might-tay VELVET STERN."

Hoots and hollers filled the room. Two twenty-
something men in black T-shirts that read VELVET:
BORN TO SHOP came out from behind the curtain
with Velvet on a stretcher, resting prettily on a
rose satin pillow. People threw confetti. A disco

ball sprayed colored lights around the ceiling. Headset Girl put her hand up to halt the cheering.

"Okay, girl." The announcer turned to Velvet. "You got the crowd itchin' to see who you're gonna pick for first dance. Give it to me straight up." Velvet smoothed her dress and squinted out at the crowd. "Is Campbell Pekarsky here?" Velvet clutched the mike.

The crowd roared, but no one came forward. "I think he's at the race car simulator!" someone yelled. "Drew Freeman?" Velvet looked embarrassed, while Headset Girl shushed the crowd. No response. On either side of the stage, the Black T-shirt Guys were doing choreographed moves in rhythm: wavy arms with fingers woven together, thunderclaps, and hitchhiking motions. The tension built up again. "Okay, then . . . I . . . pick . . ." Velvet scanned the crowd as she shaded her eyes from overhead glare.

". . . YOU."

She was pointing at Nathan.

Chapter Thirteen

All eyes were on Nathan.

Skyler couldn't believe it. Of all the boys in the room, Velvet had picked Nathan for the first dance. *Nathan!*

"Go," she whispered, but Nathan stood frozen in place.

Skyler and Julia gave him a shove, and he stumbled onto the dance floor. Velvet waited for Nathan in front of the stage, while the crowd gathered in a circle around them. Nathan looked pale as he shuffled toward Velvet, past glamorous girls in flowing gowns. What had happened to the confident jock-walk she'd taught him?

This could be his first dance ever, Skyler realized.

Clearly, it wasn't Velvet's. She casually slid her arms around Nathan's neck and smiled flirtatiously. Skyler edged closer as Nathan nervously wiped his hands on his pants. He reached for Velvet's waist, but seemed to have trouble gripping it through the layers of pink tulle. He pushed up his glasses, and tried again.

A slow ballad played, and Velvet moved closer. But Skyler could see that Nathan's arms remained rigid, keeping her at a distance. The lights dimmed and shopping bags twinkled above the crowd. As Nathan steered her like a go-kart, Velvet leaned in, trying to close the gap between them. Nathan didn't budge.

Relax your arms, Skyler begged silently.

She hadn't reviewed dancing with Nathan, figuring they'd hit the floor together and she'd coach him. Who could have ever guessed he'd be picked for first dance? Next to her, a couple girls in baby-doll dresses were giggling.

How long *was* this stupid song, anyway?

Then Velvet made a bold move: She tried to rest her curly blond head on Nathan's shoulder. Nathan looked startled. Because of the distance between them, she had to bend over — so it looked like her head was propping up his chest. Behind Velvet's back, Nathan's hands fumbled with something on his calculator watch. Skyler tried not to bite her Marvelous Mocha fingernails.

It was painful to watch.

As the dance went on, Skyler felt her mouth go dry. If only she could rescue him! But she was stuck watching from the sidelines as Nathan and Velvet stumbled through the song, a sappy number about falling in love with a photograph.

She had to do *something*.

In a burst of inspiration, Skyler pulled Julia onto the almost empty dance floor by her denim cuff. "What are you doing?" Julia whispered. "They haven't finished their —" Skyler twirled her friend into a *Dancing with the Stars*–like tango. "Just go with it," whispered Skyler. "I'm trying to distract the crowd!" Out of the corner of her eye, she saw one of the Baby Dolls pointing at her. It was working!

Unfortunately, Skyler knew only a couple of tango steps. Their dance quickly got repetitive, and the crowd turned back to Nathan and Velvet.

Not her best idea.

Headset Girl saved them. "We're gonna take the energy up," she warned. "And get this party STARTED!" A hip-hop beat pounded the room, and girls in slinky dresses stormed the dance floor, dragging guys with them. Skyler was relieved to bail out, and she and Julia sank into folding chairs.

As the floor filled up, Skyler lost sight of Nathan. She got up to look for him, snaking through a thicket of filmy dresses. She hit a knot of people gathered around, watching something. Skyler stretched her neck out for a look.

She gasped.

It was Nathan.

His body was jerking back and forth, thumbs pointed out, feet kicking. His head seemed to be rotating on a separate axis. It took Skyler a moment to realize he was *dancing*. He was so out of time with the music, it was hard to tell. Velvet backed away from him, gripping her tiara as if her head was throbbing.

"Is he dancing or barfing?" A tall jock looked baffled.

"You go, guy," yelled someone in a BORN TO SHOP baseball hat.

A girl in a silver shawl was giggling and shaking her head. The Baby Dolls were shoving each other. Brooklyn Davis looked perplexed.

"It's like a heart attack set to music," someone said.

She and Nathan were *so* dead.

Velvet slipped away, pulling a girlfriend with her. Was she going to call security and have Nathan arrested for bad dancing?

Finally, Skyler caught his eye and frowned. He looked around, surprised to see people staring at him. He slowed down, transitioning to a milder sway. Skyler frowned again, and this time he slowed to an occasional head nod.

People were still staring.

"Well." A girl in a yellow halter dress turned around. "That was un-boring."

A squad of Black T-shirt Guys hit the floor and fanned out. They broke up the stare-fest by shouting commands: "Pump it up! Bring it down low! Take it uptown!"

The crowd started dancing again, but Nathan's gyrations had changed the energy. A boy in a yellow Oxford shirt imitated Nathan's thumbs-turned-out rotation. The idea spread through the crowd like a virus, and the floor vibrated with jerky movements and flailing limbs. They were clearly making fun of Nathan, and yet . . . wasn't imitation the highest form of flattery?

Maybe not.

Skyler grabbed Nathan and pulled him off the

floor. "What were you —" She didn't know what to say. "What did you —" But he looked so miserable, she backed off. His hair was sticking up strangely, and his shirttail had come out of his pants. "I'm sorry," she ended up saying.

They moved to the side of the room. "Skyler, it's —" Nathan looked away. "It's *me* who's sorry." He kicked some pink confetti on the floor. "I know I messed up. *Exponentially*."

"No math terms," Skyler couldn't help reminding him. "Let's get some air."

Taking him by the elbow, she guided him out to the lobby. A tiled fountain was gently bubbling, surrounded by pots of flowers. They slid onto an ornate bench.

Nathan leaned over, putting his hands on his knees.

As she ran her hand across the cool tiles around the fountain, Skyler's mind raced. How do you tell someone that pointy thumbs should never, ever, be seen on a dance floor? That moving his body to music should be *prohibited* — by federal law, if necessary?

She decided to start with the upside.

"Velvet picked you for her first dance," Skyler pointed out. "You get huge props for that."

"Okay," he said uncertainly. "But —" He kicked the fountain. "I let you down." He looked unhappy. "I'm sorry. Tell me what to do."

"Well, first of all . . ." Skyler's heart raced, remembering all his slipups. "You really shouldn't . . ."

But she couldn't finish.

His eyes looked so open and eager for approval, she paused. It was funny that what he regretted was disappointing *her* — not embarrassing himself in front of a roomful of people.

"You shouldn't sweat it," Skyler said, surprising herself. "Just tone down the hitchhike thing. Dancing is really more like . . ." She looked for the right word. "Swaying. You were catching on at the end."

Nathan reached over and dipped his hand in the fountain. "That's it?" He wiped his brow, as if he'd escaped getting a detention.

They sat there for a moment, silent, listening to the tinny splash of the water.

"You'll catch on." Skyler waved her hand. As if giving Nathan dance lessons would be easy!

Suddenly, Velvet and her girl posse flounced by. Velvet blushed when she saw Nathan. "Oh, hi," she said. "Thanks for the, uh, dance." Her friends elbowed each other and giggled. "Don't leave without your giveaway bags. The wallets

114

have my picture in them." Velvet waved to Skyler as she escaped to the bathroom.

Nathan turned back to her. "You were saying?"

She grabbed his hand and pulled him toward the dance floor. She expected it to be clammy, but it was surprisingly cool.

"Dance with me," she said.

Chapter Fourteen

Two days later, there was a message on Skyler's voice mail. She listened to it while she loaded books into her locker. "Awesome party, huh?" She recognized Brooklyn's voice. "Velvet did an *amazing* job. The cash register cake was *genius*." Skyler rolled her eyes as Brooklyn continued. "Your friend Nathan seems nice. Do you think he'd want to come to my birthday party in a few weeks? I could use a few more guys. . . ."

Well!

Skyler put down her books and listened to the message again. Nathan *hadn't* gone down in flames. Brooklyn, a cool girl at another school, had invited him to a party. Maybe the Dance Floor Disaster wasn't such a deal breaker, after all. This was good news, but Skyler felt a pang of . . . *what*? No matter — Julia would be happy to hear about their success. On the way to Julia's locker, she felt a hand on her shoulder.

Skyler spun around and saw Hunter Waxman-Orloff.

"Just got back from an emergency meeting." Hunter was out of breath. Her candy-striped Oxford shirt was untucked, and the sweater tied around her neck was coming loose. She guided Skyler over to the drinking fountain. "Our band for the Valentine's Day Dance cancelled on us."

Skyler nodded, wondering why Hunter was telling her.

"Lead singer has SATs the next day." Hunter looked disgusted. "Totally forgot! How do you 'forget' the biggest test of your life? I'm already memorizing vocabulary words: *Turgid. Excoriate. Bilious*," she said. "You think that's my idea of fun?"

"Well, I —"

"Point is, the dance is two weeks away, and we're stuck." Hunter sighed. "How about the Vectors?"

Skyler gulped, almost swallowing her chewing gum. Hunter wanted to hire Nathan's band!

"The Vectors?" Skyler was stunned. "Y-you want to book them?"

"We're desperate." Hunter put her hands together, pleading. "I'm about ready to hire my dad's folk-singing trio." She shifted her briefcase to her other hand. "JOKE! You think the Vectors would be interested?" she asked. "Their demo was pretty good."

Oh no. Oh *no*.

Skyler felt nauseated, remembering she had given Hunter the wrong CD, trying to pass it off as Nathan's. The demo Hunter had heard was for a college band, not the Vectors. Skyler had been relieved that Nathan had gotten an obscure gig — the Student Health Carnival, which wasn't until spring. Playing for an educational fair was one thing; the Valentine's Day Dance was in a different league.

"Well . . ." Skyler stalled for time. "I don't know their schedule. This is pretty last minute." She had to think of something. Maybe she could just say they were booked, and not tell Nathan. Of course, she had never heard Nathan's band — maybe they were great. Odds were, though, that they weren't ready for the biggest party of the year.

Hunter looked annoyed. "Make it happen," she said. "You were the one pushing them."

"Pushing who?" Julia threw a wildly patterned arm around Skyler. Today she'd gone urban tribal in an African top and chunky amber beads. She looked at both of them. "What'd I miss?"

"We're booking the Vectors for the Valentine's Day Dance." Hunter took out her cell phone. "Crushed Popsicle blew us off."

Julia let go of Skyler, and adjusted her beaded headband. "Nathan's band?"

Skyler shot her a warning look, but Julia was busy looking for something in her bag. Skyler coughed and said, "Well — it's an idea."

"That's great!" Julia missed Skyler's signals entirely. "Nathan's going to be *psyched*."

"See?" Hunter smiled at Skyler. "Done deal. Got to run. I have figure skating, Super Sibs, and Wig & Cloak —"

Before Skyler could pull Julia aside, the bell rang. "Is that second bell?" Julia frantically stuffed a notebook into her plastic woven bag. "Yikes! I've got to talk to Brodkey before class!" In a flash, she leaped down the hall leaving Skyler stranded with her mouth open.

"JULIA!!" Skyler's yell died in the air. She was on her own.

In history class, Ms. Graber droned on about Mayan agricultural techniques, while Skyler reviewed her options. She could tell Nathan she'd gotten his band a gig, but he might be mad if he knew the Vectors had been chosen on the basis of a phony demo. Hopefully, he wouldn't find out.

Or she could *not* tell Nathan. Which was unfair, since the whole reason Nathan had agreed to a makeover was to get the band gigs. The Valentine's Day Dance was the holy grail, the ultimate make-or-break event. But she'd already got them the Health Carnival gig, and besides, she had never even heard their music. Could she risk a high-profile performance that was anything less than awesome? If they bombed, how could she success-fully present Nathan as a cool guy and win her bet with Madison?

The best thing was *not* to tell him.

She'd make up a phony story for Hunter, say-ing the band had another gig. That way she couldn't get in trouble and Nathan's band wouldn't be under pressure. She'd spend the next two weeks concentrating on Nathan's dazzling debut. After he was anointed a cool guy, *then* she'd help him find gigs. She opened her ancient civilizations textbook, relieved to have a plan.

When the bell rang, Skyler had her backpack on her shoulder, ready to find Hunter in the lunch-room. She scanned the room for her frizzy head, when something almost knocked her over.

"Hey." Nathan pounded on her shoulder from behind. "Great job! High five." He raised his hand expectantly, waiting for her to match it.

What?

"Ran into Julia just now." He was out of breath. "She said another band cancelled, so the Vectors got the Valentine's Day gig. That's *awesome*."

If only she'd gotten to Julia first and told her not to spill the news!

"A jillion thanks, obviously." He squeezed her shoulder. "You really went to bat for us."

"Yeah, well." So much for her big plan. "Listen," she said. "I ought to come by your practice session. See how it sounds." She had a bad feeling about this.

"No prob. After school, Jasper's garage," he said. "Yellow house at the end of Orchard Street. Gotta go." He put his fist up to bump knuckles, and Skyler lifted her hand halfheartedly. He pointed across the lunchroom. "Comics trading powwow. Annihilator #45 is within reach." He ran off, and turned back to look at her a few steps later. "You're the BEST!"

"Yeah, yeah." Skyler waved. If he only knew she wasn't even going to tell him about it!

He disappeared into the lunchroom chaos, and Skyler slumped at the table. *Don't panic*, she warned herself. Maybe the band wasn't so bad . . . they could be decent, right? Maybe Nathan wouldn't find out how he got the gig. *This will all work out*, she told herself. She stretched her neck around to locate Julia.

Instead, Madison and Sienna walked up and put down their trays.

"We never see you anymore." Madison brushed blond hair out of her eyes. Today she was dressed tomboy glam in a sequined beret and leopard-print vest. "Your science experiment is looking better, I have to admit." Skyler winced at Madison's words, then realized she had referred to Nathan that way herself a few weeks ago. "Looks like he got new safety goggles."

Skyler managed a half smile, and took the lid off her yogurt. She wasn't in the mood for Madison's digs. Sienna giggled, her blond curls spilling over her blue mohair turtleneck sweater.

"'Course, he's far from being *Ashleigh Carr*–worthy." Madison's voice was lazy, stretching out the name. "You're not still thinking Ashleigh's going to ask him to dance, are you? That would be delusional." Madison took out a clear plastic carton of sushi rolls. "Wasn't her last boyfriend, like, in high school?"

Skyler could feel anger rise in her chest. *Play it cool*, she told herself.

"I'm not wigging." Skyler shrugged. "In fact, this bet is such a slam dunk, I already have an outfit for my victory party." She daintily scooped out fruit from the bottom of her yogurt. "Goth surfer jumper, paired with chain-link necklace." It was important to show she had no intention of losing the bet.

"Planning ahead, are we?" Madison's voice dripped with sarcasm. "If I were you, I'd be putting together *his* outfit, not yours. Last time I checked, *Teen Vogue* didn't show purple plastic capes." Sienna giggled again.

"I'm SO not worried about Nathan." Skyler licked her yogurt spoon. Should she tell them about Nathan's success at Velvet's party? No — better not tip her hand. "In fact, I'll be surprised if Ashleigh doesn't ask him out."

Madison and Sienna collapsed into laughter, clutching their stomachs.

"Oh, *that'll* happen." Madison gasped. "I'll be holding my breath. Too bad you'll have to give up running for Fashion Club prez. Don't even THINK about bailing on our bet."

Skyler grabbed her backpack with one hand

and her tray in another. As Julia headed toward the table with her tray, Skyler motioned for her to turn around. This bet had brought out the worst in Madison, and her jabs were really getting Skyler down. Why hadn't she ever seriously told her to get lost? Why did everyone put up with her?

But that was the Madison Problem — she was so popular, no one dared to challenge her. Well, on Valentine's Day, she'd put Madison in her place. Skyler slammed her lunch tray on another table, while Julia sat down next to her.

She HAD to win this bet.

Madison Gillette was going *down*.

Chapter Fifteen

She heard them before she saw them.

The yellow house on Orchard Street wasn't hard to find. It was a Victorian three-story with a sagging porch and leftover Christmas lights. As Skyler followed the driveway to the garage, she was assaulted by an earsplitting jangle of guitars, thumping drums, and the sound of digitized laser fire.

Please, let that be the Vectors warming up, thought Skyler. *Let it be some kind of feedback problem.*

Please, God, don't let that be a SONG.

She knocked on the side door of the garage. No answer. She knocked again, but nobody heard. Finally, she pushed the door open.

Since the garage was unheated, the Vectors were bundled up. Nathan was drumming furiously on a set of covered bowls. Jasper's scratchy scarf grazed the floor while he played lead guitar. A skinny guy in a down vest over surgical scrubs was blowing into a garden hose with a funnel on it. A boy with wild black hair stuffed into a Chicago Black Hawks ski cap was at the control board. Next to him was the slight, olive-skinned girl, banging a fork on a row of soda bottles, each one filled with a different amount of liquid.

What in the world . . . ?

Skyler recognized the girl from the comics trading session in the park a few weeks ago. How long ago that seemed! Now the girl was playing her water bottles like a xylophone. The guy at the mixer then distorted those sounds electronically. It was too weird.

Then Nathan started singing.

"MOUTH OF METAL, HEART OF GOLD . . ."

He barely nodded at Skyler, as if he were in a deep, musical trance. The instruments were mind-numbingly loud, like they were colliding with one another. The xylophone tones added an eerie note, along with what sounded like video game sounds. *Like a car wreck inside a Nintendo game*, thought Skyler.

The music was strange, provocative, and possibly even cool — but definitely *not* what you'd want to dance to at the Valentine's Day Dance.

When the screeching stopped, Jasper and Nathan looked at her expectantly. "Well," said Nathan, "how do we sound?"

All eyes were on her. "Wow, that was . . ." Skyler shook her head. "WOW."

"Yeah, today it really came together." Jasper brushed back his long blond hair. "But, honestly, we don't always nail it."

Skyler wondered what an "off" day was like.

"It's called 'Ode to Missing Dental Appliances,'" added Jasper.

"Wow." Skyler elbowed Nathan. "Introduce me."

He jumped up immediately. "Hey, guys, this is Skyler — the one who got us this gig." Scrubs Guy banged on a flowerpot with a spoon to applaud her.

Nathan looked around the room. "You know Jasper." He pointed with a drumstick. Jasper nodded and strummed his guitar. "Melinger," Nathan continued, and Scrubs Guy saluted. "Khalid," he pointed at the guy at the mixer. "And Absinthia." Absinthia stood up and smiled shyly, giving Skyler a better view of her baggy jeans and off-brand gym shoes. "Teachers call me Marcy," she said.

"We're sampling sounds from early video games." Khalid pushed levers on the control board. "Neat, huh?"

"Check out our homemade instruments." Nathan pointed to his drums. "Bowls covered with balloons." He held up mallets with marbled rubber tips. "Drumsticks made from SuperBalls and dowels."

Pretty creative, she had to admit.

"It's hard to label us," said Jasper. "Obviously, we're influenced by bands like Self Dentistry and Conjunctivitis."

"Obviously." Skyler had never heard of them.

"But we're not just another No Wave, psychobilly, alt-noise mash-up."

"I'd *never* call you that," said Skyler.

"Atypical instruments, ironic wordplay." Nathan shook a plastic food container filled with beans. "That's what we're known for."

This was a complete disaster.

"Guys." Skyler leaned on an amp, careful not to wrinkle her pink-and-black-checkered jumper. "Do you know any, uh, *regular* songs?"

"Lots." Jasper plucked his guitar for emphasis. "You should hear all the stuff we've written."

"No." Skyler's voice was sharp. "NOT songs

you've written. Songs people *know* already."
Everyone looked up at her, alarmed at her new
tone of voice.

Jasper looked angry, and Nathan looked
worried. "We're doing something different here,"
said Jasper. "We're not some sellout, pop-music
clone show."

Deep breath.

"I have to be honest with you." Skyler
shook her head. "If you play what I just heard,
you're going to bomb on Valentine's Day. It's . . .
interesting music, but it won't fly for a school
dance. No way." There — she'd said it.

The garage was uncomfortably silent.

"People want something catchy, something
they can dance to." She lifted her chin. "Mainstream
songs — hits they know already." Skyler men-
tioned a singer who had performed at the Super
Bowl halftime show.

"I HATE that guy," said Jasper, and Nathan,
Melinger, and Absinthia all nodded.

"My sister reads these moronic magazines."
Jasper put on a girl's voice. "Fave car, pizza topping, innie or outie —" Everyone rolled their eyes
in disgust.

"Innie," Khalid said quietly.

"Boxers or briefs —" Jasper barreled on, and then stopped. He turned to look at Khalid. "*What* did you say?"

"He's an innie." He shrugged. "If you want to get technical about it."

"The guy is —" Jasper started, and then turned to Khalid again. "How did you know that?"

Khalid sipped from his juice box. "My sister gets *Teen Beat.*"

Skyler smiled at him gratefully. Who would have guessed this scruffy music geek read "Facts 'n Faves" lists?

"I can't believe we're *talking* about this!" Jasper's voice cracked. "Why does she get to tell us what to do?" He motioned toward Skyler, and looked at the other guys for support. Melinger blew on his garden hose.

Nathan left the drum set and came over to Skyler. "Uh — time-out, guys." He held up his hand. "Skyler and I need to interface —" She gave him a look. "Talk, I mean." He put down his drumsticks and led Skyler down the driveway. Skyler waved at the group, but only Absinthia waved back.

They walked around to the front of the house, and Skyler leaned against a tree. "Lots of our songs are danceable," Nathan said, upset. "It's just not the usual boy-group stuff they're used to."

He wasn't getting it.

"Nathan, this dance is *really* important — for you, for everyone." Skyler pulled her silver-and-pink ski jacket tighter around her. "I'm not helping you by sending you up there unprepared. Do yourself a favor — cancel the gig. They can hire someone else." She dreaded telling Hunter, but what choice did she have?

"Are you kidding?" Nathan was shocked. "This is a primo opportunity for us," he continued. "No *way* would we give it up. I can't believe you would ask us to!"

Skyler picked a piece of bark off the tree. It made her miserable to tell Nathan to pull out of the show. But what else could she do? Up until now, he had been unpopular but unknown. Bombing at the dance would make him unpopular and *famous*. Her stomach felt queasy, thinking about it.

"Nathan, listen." She twisted her scarf around her hands. "It's not that I don't *like* your music — I do! But the crowd will be expecting something else."

"Why do you think I *agreed* to this whole make-me-over thing?" Nathan shot back. "So the band could get gigs! We need this break. The crowd's going to like it. I *know* they will." Skyler pictured the Vectors in the school gym, playing water-bottle xylophones and banging on flowerpots, with Madison and Kyle looking on in horror.

"Nathan, I'm the one on the inside here." Skyler's voice was pleading. "You've never even *been* to a dance! You want to get booed offstage?"

"Not gonna happen." He folded his arms.

"I only want what's best for you!" Skyler cried.

"Then lay off," Nathan spat out. "THAT'S what's best for me!"

Skyler stomped away, furious.

She fumed as she marched down Orchard Street. Didn't they want the same thing — for him to succeed at the Valentine's Day Dance? True, their definitions of success were slightly different. Nathan didn't know that for Skyler, success meant Nathan getting Ashleigh Carr's attention — and winning her bet with Madison. But she had made the bet to prove that anyone could be cool, and Nathan would be all over *that* idea.

Provided, of course, she had actually told him.

By the time she'd gotten to the end of the block, she had managed to push away the little voice reminding her she hadn't been totally honest. How dare he refuse her advice? Who did Nathan Stillman think he was, anyway?

Chapter Sixteen

As she sat in biology lab, Skyler tried to put the fight with Nathan out of her mind. It made her miserable to remember his face after she said they should cancel the gig. She thought she'd been right to be honest with him: If the Vectors played, the Valentine's Day crowd would boo them off the stage.

Still, it was hard to deny she was responsible for the situation.

"First, you want to determine the sex of your frog...." Her science teacher, Mr. Izbicky, was going on in his enthusiastic, gee-isn't-it-cool way. He was a short, balding guy with rimless glasses, known for wearing holiday-themed neckties. "Look at the thumb pads on the front feet."

Kyle Townshend, Skyler's new lab partner, peered at the pale gray creature on a metal tray. "It's a dude."

"Now take your scalpel and make an incision from the throat to where the legs meet," said the teacher.

"This loser's getting WHOMPED." Kyle pumped his fist.

It took Skyler a second to realize he meant the frog.

Getting assigned to Kyle was a stroke of luck. When lab partners were announced, the other girls had been openly jealous. "It's not fair," Sienna Goldblum had grumbled, when she got assigned to oddball Becca Frost. Skyler knew how Sienna felt: If you *had* to slice open a frog, better to look at Kyle while you did it.

His blond hair, athletic body, and backward baseball cap were certainly easy on the eyes. And while he wasn't the best student, he seemed very fond of frogs. If Skyler played him right, maybe she could get him to do the actual dissecting.

"Scalpel." He held out his hand, and Skyler made like a nurse.

"Pull back the skin flaps, and look at the

frog's abdominal muscles." Izbicky pointed to a diagram.

"Check out his six-pack." Kyle peeled back the skin. "Not as good as mine." He lifted his soccer jersey and patted himself proudly.

Skyler looked at Kyle's rippled stomach. "Wow." It was a nice distraction from the poor frog. "How often do you work out?"

"Twenty hours a week." Kyle's voice was lazy. "I can bench-press most sixth graders."

That was a lot of time lifting weights. Skyler's mind strayed to Nathan, who filled his time with more interesting activities. With a pang, she remembered his room, overflowing with books, maps, and souvenirs.

"Maybe not really FAT guys," Kyle conceded.

Izbicky explained that frogs store fat inside the body cavity. "Does anyone know what frogs order at McDonald's? Burgers and flies!" Everyone groaned. "You could also tell that joke with spiders," he added. "They eat flies, too."

"Except for Spider-Man." Skyler remembered something Nathan had told her. Did she actually say that out loud?

"You read Spider-Man?" Kyle raised an eyebrow.

"No." Skyler shook her head. "Someone told me. You know Nathan Stillman?"

"Dude with the cape?" Kyle snorted. "I could bench-press HIM, no problem."

"He's really into comics." Skyler rolled her eyes. "Goes to conventions, knows all the artists and writers." Kyle was now lifting up the heart to find the esophagus.

She stopped herself from mentioning he had an edition of Rat Girl worth two hundred dollars.

"Nathan." Kyle looked like he suddenly remembered something. "Yeah. He has fungus growing in his backpack. The custodian won't even go near his locker. This one time? He ate a worm at lunch!"

Skyler's jaw dropped.

"What?" She pulled away. "Where did you hear that?"

"Dunno. Slam book, maybe?" Kyle shrugged, probing the frog. "The SPHINCTER," he announced loudly. "AWESOME." He high-fived a guy at a neighboring table.

Someone was spreading lies about Nathan! Skyler stood up and put a hand on his shoulder. "Kyle, the stuff you said about Nathan was totally bogus." She looked him straight in the eye. "I *have* to know where you read it."

Kyle scowled and scooped out the esophagus, stomach, and intestines. "Someone passed around a notebook." He wiped his hand. "Glittery stuff on the cover. Don't remember who."

Maybe he didn't.

But Skyler did.

The girls' bathroom on the second floor was the gathering place for cool seventh grade girls. When Skyler walked in, Jameeka Lacewell was applying lip liner, dressed like a 1960s British rocker in a ruffled blouse and oversize men's jacket. Sienna Goldblum had gone gypsy-fairy in a lacy top and fringed shawl, with high lace-up boots. She was at the mirror, scrunching her blond curls with the concentration of a heart surgeon.

"The directions say, 'rinse, finger fluff, and go.'" Sienna pouted. "But my hair is *still* flat."

Jameeka nodded sympathetically. "Try towel-drying it." She dabbed her lips with raspberry-colored gloss.

Skyler suppressed a smile. The usual issues of crucial importance.

"Killer outfits, guys." Skyler glanced at them as she turned to the mirror to touch up her mascara. "Say. Does anyone know where that slam book is? The one with the glittery cover?"

Sienna and Jameeka looked at each other slyly. "Don't know," said Sienna, moving on to face powder.

"Uh-huh." Skyler combed her lashes upward. "'Cause I really need to find it."

"Sounds mysterious." Sienna dusted her cheeks with a pink-tipped brush.

"Naw, I'm just . . ." Skyler had to find the right tone here. "Curious."

More sounds of hair brushing, plastic cases opening, a mascara wand being pumped.

Time to play hardball. Skyler fumbled in her bag, and pulled out a keychain with a famous monkey on it. "Say, can either of you guys use a key chain?" she said. "Turns out I have two."

Not true, but she could always get another one.

If she ever went to New York again.

"Sure." Jameeka shrugged. She took the leather key chain, but didn't volunteer information. "Those are neat." Sienna looked at Skyler's armful of bangle bracelets. "Do they come as a set?"

No, not the bangles! They were a gift from Julia!

Sienna and Jameeka resumed looking in the mirror.

Skyler reluctantly removed half the bracelets. "Take," she commanded. "I have so many they weigh my arm down."

Sienna accepted them happily, while Skyler jiggled her skimpy wrist. The effect was wrong unless you had a whole armful. With a sigh, she removed the remaining bracelets and put them on the sink next to Sienna.

"Guys?" Skyler was getting impatient. *"Slam book?"*

"Okay, okay." Jameeka nodded at Sienna, as if sensing Skyler's limit. "Trilby Dodson has it."

"Trilby, thanks." Skyler tried to act unhurried as she gave her hair a few extra pats. A couple sixth grade girls came into the bathroom, snapping gum and laughing loudly. She waved to Jameeka and Sienna, lingering in a leisurely way, until the door had swung shut.

And then she bolted down the hall.

Skyler found Trilby in the gym locker room.

"Do you have . . . ?" Skyler lowered her voice. "I heard you had a, um . . ." It was hard to get the words out. " . . . slam book?"

"Sky-LER!" Trilby said her name like a football chant, putting down a towel to bump knuckles. Trilby was a girls' soccer star, tall and athletic.

She reached into a mesh drawstring bag with a soccer ball. "Please take it away," begged Trilby, handing her a glitter notebook with stickers of hearts and bows. "This book is *nasty*."

So everyone hates this book, thought Skyler. *But everyone writes in it.*

Skyler went to the library to examine the book in private. Only hard-core nerds used the library at lunch, and Mrs. Wolfe, the librarian, was clearly pleased to see her there. She was a slender woman with a silver topknot who wore big glasses and carried public radio tote bags. "Finding what you need?" she asked hopefully.

"All set." Skyler waved the glitter notebook. Mrs. Wolfe frowned.

Skyler crossed the room and planted her backpack at a desk under a sign that read SCIENCE REFERENCE: M–Z.

No one would find her *there*.

The book looked vaguely familiar, with its confusing jumble of sloppy handwriting and different colored pens. Sometimes words snaked around the edges of a page or crammed into corners. Smiley faces, hearts, and other doodles dotted the pages.

She skimmed the book for Nathan's name. There was a list of fashion disasters, and a

140

section marked *Dweebs to Watch Out For*. She didn't look too hard at the slams; reading them made her uneasy. Someone ranted about seventh grade guys not being as good-looking as eighth grade guys. A sleepover party got a bad review.

Then she saw it.

In Madison's handwriting, of course.

Does anyone know a Superdork named Nathan Stillman? it said. *This guy is so nerdy he should be banned from Longbrook. He has REAL problems with personil hygiene, and once the janitor had to clean up his own barf after seeing what was in Nathan's locker — so he won't go near it any-more. True story, a friend of a friend of mine saw it. He's been known to eat stuff from the science lab for lunch, worms, and even parts of lab rats and . . .*

Skyler made a giant X through the page and wrote *LIES* in big letters.

Madison was evil.

She shut the book, fuming. But after a few minutes, she opened it again. Was there more stuff about Nathan? She braced herself, flipping through the pages, until she was ambushed by something familiar. . . .

Her own handwriting.

141

She had written a page called "Fashion Court," listing the criminal, crime, verdict, and suggested punishment. She had convicted Lily Perotta for "Miniskirt Abuse," Jenna Fingerman for "Mixing Animal Prints," and Francine Otto for "Being Francine Otto." Seeing her words scrawled across the page made Skyler feel nauseated. What had she been *thinking*?

The entry that made her most ashamed was about Sanjay. He was a shy kid who had transferred to Longbrook in the middle of the year, and didn't have many friends. Life for him was probably tough enough without having his clothes dissed in a stupid slam book. Before she'd met Nathan, nerdy guys like that were just background scenery, not real people with feelings, hopes, and comic book collections. She cringed when she read her entry about him.

FASHION COURT

Criminal: *Sanjay Ghosh*
Crime: *Wearing black loafers with tube socks*
Verdict: *Guilty*
Suggested punishment: *De-loafer and flog with own fanny pack*

She shut the book sadly.

I'm sorry, Sanjay, thought Skyler. *You seem like a nice guy; I don't know why I wrote that.*

Seeing her own words took some of the strength out of her indignation at Madison. Skyler had been snarky, too, making fun of easy targets. Madison had gone further, telling outright lies. But Skyler couldn't exactly claim the high ground.

Nice work.

She slammed the book shut and tore out of the desk, waving to Mrs. Wolfe.

"Don't forget the book fair!" the librarian called to her with a smile. Something about her hopeful reminder made Skyler even sadder, knowing she probably wouldn't go. She felt like she was doomed to let everyone down: Sanjay, Nathan, even the librarian. As Skyler opened the thick glass door, it felt extra heavy.

She'd been furious at Madison — and she still was. But she was even more furious at herself.

Was it too late to change?

Chapter Seventeen

Skyler knew just where to find her.

Madison and Sienna were sitting on benches near the front of the cafeteria, rating people's outfits as they walked by. Sienna looked like a wilted angel in her gypsy blouse and Victorian boots, while Madison rocked a pin-striped vest over a tuxedo shirt and jeans.

"Eight point four." Madison turned her head to admire a soccer player's sherbet-colored polo shirt. Neither girl realized Skyler was standing next to them. "Three point five." Sienna appraised a smock-waist top.

"Hey, Madison." Skyler's tone was casual. "Written lies in any slam books lately?"

Madison and Sienna looked up, startled.

"Eats worms for lunch? Janitor barfs near his locker?" Skyler folded her arms. "Give me a freakin' break!"

Skyler watched as Madison decided to be amused. "Well, aren't *we* defensive?" Madison exchanged glances with Sienna.

"Nathan's locker isn't a toxic waste site," Skyler said sharply. "And he's not a slob. In fact, his room is so neat that —" As soon as the words were out of her mouth, Skyler realized her mistake.

"You saw his *bedroom*?" Sienna squealed happily. "Wow . . . this is serious." Madison and Sienna giggled. What, were they six years old?

Suddenly, Skyler just felt weary. She sank onto the bench, planting her hobo bag next to her.

"Look, I've written in slam books before —" said Skyler.

"True that." Madison lifted her chin defiantly. "So who are *you* to talk?"

"Madison, I —" Skyler began. "I'm not proud of it. I didn't think about people's feelings." But that was before she got to know Nathan.

"And I should care because . . . ?" Madison's tone was sarcastic.

Skyler was about to fling back something angry, but she stopped herself. She really wanted to get through to Madison, not just have a catfight.

"Nathan's cool," she said quietly. "He deserves better. Give him a chance to prove himself."

"Don't get your boy shorts in a twist." Madison waved. "If he's so great, he'll prove me wrong." She fluffed up the ruffles on her tuxedo blouse. "We both know this is about the bet."

"No way, Madison," Skyler insisted. "This is about Nathan — *not* about the bet."

"Bet?" Skyler heard Nathan's voice. "What bet?"

Nathan was standing right in front of them.

Skyler felt her blood freeze.

Nathan's eyes moved from Skyler to Madison. His hair was tousled, and his blue Oxford shirt was wrinkled, as if he'd gotten dressed in a hurry. A computer cable dangled from an open zipper on his backpack. Skyler, Madison, and Sienna all stood up.

Skyler rubbed her forehead and sighed.

Talk about *bad timing*.

Madison smiled sweetly at Nathan. "Your 'friend' here made a bet she could pass you off as one of us. If she wins, she gets to be Fashion Club prez. Ask her about it." She picked up a purse that looked like a doctor's satchel, and Sienna threw her shawl over her shoulder. They strode out of the lunchroom, leaving Skyler and Nathan standing alone.

Nathan looked stunned.

"You made a bet about me?" Nathan shook his head. "I don't get it."

Things were so wrecked, she didn't even know where to begin. "Nathan, I . . ." Her voice faded. "It's not how it . . ."

Rats.

Rats.

Rats.

"You get to be president of some club?" Nathan squinted. "Because of —"

"It's a really long story." Skyler felt her cheeks get hot. She shifted her weight. "Why don't we go somewhere and —"

"Can't." Nathan pulled out a CD in a plastic case, and pressed a crumpled note into Skyler's hand. "I came over to ask you about this. Hunter gave it to me."

She unfolded it clumsily, aching with dread.

Nathan —
Here's your Vectors CD back. Can u believe dance is next week?
Hunter

As she read the note, Skyler's hands started to shake.

Now her life was — officially — over.

Nathan took the note and CD out of her hand. He turned over the disk, which was unlabeled. "Skyler." His words were slow and serious. "What *is* this?"

Her worst nightmare, pretty much.

She took a deep breath. "I gave Hunter someone else's demo CD to get you the gig. I don't know what I was thinking."

He stared at her in disbelief. The silence was excruciating. *Yell at me*, she thought. He had to say something — *anything*!

"If you needed a demo, why didn't you just ask me?" Nathan was trembling.

No good answer to that.

"You really don't trust me at all, do you?" Nathan sounded like he was slowly starting to grasp something. "Did it ever occur to you that maybe, just *maybe*, I'd be able to do it? Or that at least I deserved the chance to try?"

Skyler stared at her feet miserably.

He shook his head again. "And to think I was going to apologize because I felt bad about our fight. I thought we were friends."

"We *are*!" Skyler lifted her head. "I'm —"

"Not anymore." Nathan's voice broke. "Because now, I don't trust *you*."

Skyler watched him heave the backpack over his shoulder and walk to the far end of the cafeteria. His body got smaller and smaller until he blended into the crowd.

He didn't look back.

Chapter Eighteen

For the next week, Skyler tried to run into Nathan to set things right. But he wasn't in any of his usual places — the far end of the lunchroom, the park, tech lab. She started seeing more of her "cool" table buddies, which meant more of Madison. Since their confrontation, though, Skyler was careful to avoid one-on-one conversations. Their shaky friendship had become an open rivalry now, with a showdown set for Valentine's Day.

Hopefully, Nathan would stick to their deal.

Would he still go along with her Cool Guy rules? Maybe he had gone back to wearing his silver galactic warlord jacket and combing his hair like a rooster. Wistfully, she wondered what he was doing. Playing drums? Drawing storyboards? Designing a spaceport?

Skyler's new, Nathan-less life left more time to shop, talk on the phone, and plan her Valentine's Day outfit. She ought to be grateful! If things had gone as planned, she'd be going crazy this week, getting Nathan ready for the big event: reviewing clothes, conversation, dancing. Instead, she had time on her hands.

Too much time.

"How much do you love my dress?" asked Julia.

Skyler was sprawled on the bed in her friend's bedroom, leaning against a plush, quilted headboard. Julia liked her bedroom to look like a swanky hotel room, with zebra chairs and a mod 60s steel lamp. She was standing in front of her closet, holding up what looked like a pile of hot-pink feathers.

"That's a *dress*?" Skyler crawled over for a better look. The feathers were attached to a slinky tube of fabric.

"It's my psychedelic flapper look." Julia admired the dress in the mirror. "Isn't it original?"

"Mmmm," said Skyler.

"I love the one-shouldered thing," said Julia.

There was a time Julia wouldn't have bought a dress for a major occasion without consulting her, Skyler thought. Her fashion sense had always been playful, but lately it was downright wild — mixing

151

metallic pants and a crocheted vest, a suede patchwork jacket and a pillbox hat. Julia was branching out, finding her own sense of style. Although Skyler wouldn't be caught dead in Julia's outfit, she was impressed.

"It came with a sash." Julia tilted her head. "But a red glitter belt might look more Valentine's Day-ish."

"Wow," Skyler said. "You *go*, girl."

The next day at Fashion Club, Skyler found herself thinking rebellious thoughts. Maybe Julia's fashion pluck had infected her. About twenty-five well-dressed girls were packed into the classroom, a smaller group than usual. Several members of the Valentine's Day Dance committee — including Ashleigh and Julia — were absent. They were in the gym, decorating for the big day.

Sienna was up front addressing the club. "We have a few things on the agenda." She wore a plaid flannel minidress with a denim jacket and dozens of necklaces. "A sign-up sheet to work on our newsletter, *Clothes Calls*. A petition for more flattering gym suits. And later, we'll do a Handbag Horoscope."

Jameeka raised her hand. "Don't forget —"

Sienna nodded. "Today's report: 'Eco-Friendly Lip Gloss.'"

The meeting continued with the usual discussion of this week's fashion heroes and victims, supported by helpful photos from *Teen People*. A singing star was slammed for mixing tweed and strappy sandals; a model applauded for a clingy beaded gown. Then the examples became more local.

"Speaking of fashion don'ts." Maya Benitez tossed back long, dark hair. "What is *with* the wacko outfits Julia's wearing lately?"

Skyler's head snapped up. Sometimes there was gossip at meetings, but criticism of other members was rare. Right now Julia was at the gym, hanging paper cupids from the ceiling. When had *she* fallen out of favor with the group?

"What do you . . . ?" Skyler sputtered. "I think she looks *great*."

Sienna and Madison exchanged glances, while Maya continued. "Usually I like the whole tomboy-girly thing, but . . . cowboy boots and legwarmers? Hel-LO?"

Hmmm. That *was* hard to defend, but . . .

Suddenly, everyone was chiming in.

"Last week she wore a belt that looked like my grandmother's orthopedic brace!"

"Harem pants —"

"Knickers with fringe!"

Skyler listened to the Julia-bashing with disbelief. Julia was everyone's friend — and her best friend. The attack was so unexpected, Skyler just sat there, stunned by each new accusation. Some new line had been crossed here . . . or did it just seem that way because it was Julia they were dumping on? They wouldn't dare do this in front of Ashleigh.

"Guys." Skyler got on her feet. "Will everyone just *shut up*?"

The other girls looked up, jolted by her outburst.

"This is *Julia* you're criticizing." Skyler put her hands on her hips. "Organizer of the Earring Swap. Inventor of Backward Day!"

Madison was impatient. "We appreciate those things, but we're the *Fashion* Club. We have to hold everyone to a high standard."

"Really?" Skyler's palms were sweating. "I thought the club was about sharing ideas — not getting on someone's case for being different."

"We've criticized people's clothes before." Jameeka lifted an eyebrow. "You were happy to pitch in."

"Yeah, I did." Skyler remembered the slam book entry and felt ashamed. "Somehow I — maybe, all of us — got on the wrong track. Fashion

154

should be about creativity and taking risks." Skyler looked at the colorful classroom. "*Not* judging."

Angry buzzing followed — and a few murmurs of approval.

"I didn't know we were making campaign speeches today." Madison stood up, smoothing down her white shirt and men's necktie. "Skyler and I have different visions of the club. My goal is to raise this school's fashion IQ and promote excellence, not sloppiness."

Skyler felt something stir inside her. If she were Fashion Club president, she could set a new tone for the club, maybe even the school. Make it less about judging others, and more about, well, fashion. Help people play by their own rules.

Just like Nathan always had.

Then it hit Skyler: Nathan *should* play his oddball music on Valentine's Day. Julia *had* to wear that crazy dress. And Skyler needed to be true to herself, too, whether that meant defending her best friend, playing the flute, or creating a better Fashion Club.

Unfortunately, the only way to remake Fashion Club was to win the bet with Madison.

Skyler pulled her hobo bag over her shoulder and grabbed her sweater.

She knew what she had to do.

Chapter Nineteen

It was the day of the big dance, and Skyler still hadn't reached Nathan. Texting and leaving phone messages brought no response.

After Fashion Club on Thursday, she had even swallowed her pride and gone straight to his house. Her heart pounded as she rang the doorbell, but no answer. Shivering in the cold, she even went around the back of the house to look at his bedroom window. The room was dark, and she couldn't see anything but a peeling Superman decal on the glass.

Now it was noon on Saturday, the day of the dance, and Skyler tried one more time. *"Hey, it's Nathan. I'm not here right now. Leave your digits at the sound of the explosion —"*

She hung up.

Was there any way to let him know before the dance that she had been wrong? Would he even talk to her? Was winning the bet with Madison still possible, when it was suddenly more important than *ever*?

She couldn't stand the suspense.

In the meantime, she had serious work to do, starting with a call to Julia. It took less than two hours to decide on hair (full and bouncy for Skyler, tousled for Julia), nails (French manicure for Skyler, red for Julia), and coats (Skyler's mom's faux fur, and Julia's hooded cape — with both of them praying it didn't rain or snow).

Skyler didn't tell Julia what her so-called friends at Fashion Club had said about her clothes. She was proud of Julia for wearing her daring, kooky outfits — more power to her. If Skyler did get to be head of Fashion Club, she'd make Julia vice president.

Or at least shoe czar.

Saturday afternoon, Skyler's bathroom turned into a beauty spa: lavender bubble bath, green-tea face mask, and mani-pedi-rama. Pores were squeezed, skin was softened. Hair was washed, conditioned, towel-dried, misted, scrunched, combed, pinned, moussed, shined, spritzed, and shaken into glamorous, messy waves. It took a lot of time to look like you just rolled out of bed.

And then there was the Dress.

Skyler pulled the plastic wrapping back and fingered the layers of red glitter tulle held up by delicate spaghetti straps. She slipped it on, admiring the red silk waistband and sparkly bodice. To complete the va-va-voom look, she clipped a red silk flower behind her ear. With her mother's pearl bracelet, she looked like a human valentine.

Perfect.

She tried Nathan again — no answer. Shouldn't he be getting dressed now? Was he putting on the chinos she'd picked out for him? How about that blue woven shirt that brought out his eyes? And was he tousling his hair the way she'd showed him to? Did he remember not to wear white socks?

All she could do now was pray.

When Skyler walked into the gym with Julia, she felt transported. Giant glittery red letters spelled out VALENTINE'S DAY DANCE, amid clusters of red and pink balloons tied with silver curling ribbon. Red cupids, paper hearts, and pink and white streamers dangled from the ceiling. The electronic scoreboard was dripping with silver tinsel. Glass jars with candles lit the room with a soft glow, transforming the gym into a red-white-and-pink fantasy.

As she floated inside, she felt something hit her head. What in the world . . . ? A red cardboard cupid fell off the wall and hit her like a missile. The jolt threw her off balance for a moment, and dusted her arms with fine red glitter. She and Julia exchanged a well-*that*-was-weird look.

Skyler brushed herself off as they made their way to the snack table. On the way, people turned and stared. Skyler was flattered; maybe her walking-valentine look was causing a stir! Then she realized they were looking at Julia, or rather, Julia's dress.

Her best friend lit up the room in a blast of hot-pink feathers. Silver Mardi Gras beads added extra shimmer, along with a black patent wrist bag on a chunky chain. Sheer white hose and high-heeled Mary Janes gave her a touch of elegance. Though Skyler hadn't loved the dress at first, with the accessories, it was dazzling. Some of Julia's recent experiments had Skyler scratching her head, but this one totally hit the mark.

"Wow," said Jameeka, who wore red shirred silk. "I didn't know hot pink came that hot."

"Can I touch the fluff?" squealed Sienna. "Oooh!"

"I hope you're not shedding," sniffed Maya Benitez. As Julia's loudest critic, she seemed annoyed by the buzz. Maya was sulking around, sidelined in a forgettable coral chiffon.

Julia was clearly enjoying the attention. "Thanks," she said happily, patting her head to make sure the red bows were in place. "I always wanted a hot-pink feather boa. So I thought: Why not have a whole dress like that?"

While her best friend was holding court, Skyler checked out the table covered in red paper and white doilies. Glass jars held assorted candies: Atomic Fireballs, Red Hots, Hershey Kisses, red M&M's, and candy hearts. White flowers floated in a bowl of red fruit punch. A giant piñata shaped like a pair of lips hung above the table, and red glow-necklaces hung around people's necks.

At the end of the room was a raised platform, since the gym doubled as an auditorium. The stage was decorated with silver garlands, and more red and pink balloons. The heavy beige curtains were closed, but they flared out occasionally to reveal people moving around behind them.

That's where Nathan is, she realized.

She swallowed.

She slid between clusters of girls in faux fur, satin, and lace, into the hallway that led backstage. When she reached the stage door, Skyler nearly collided with Ms. Fortunato, her gym teacher, standing guard with a clipboard. She wore a warm-up suit, gym shoes, and — a nod to Valentine's Day? — a red baseball cap.

"No one's allowed backstage."

"I need to talk to Nathan Stillman," Skyler begged.

"Why?"

"I have an important message."

Fortunato shook her head.

"He's wanted by Homeland Security," Skyler said.

Fortunato gave her a look.

Skyler tried again. "His sister REALLY needs his kidney."

Fortunato folded her arms.

"His pet tarantula is missing?" Skyler was running out of ideas.

Fortunato didn't budge.

"*Pleeeease*," Skyler begged. "It's a matter of life and death!"

Fortunato folded her arms.

"Fine!" said Skyler, waving her red purse wildly. "But don't say I didn't warn —" She didn't finish

161

her sentence, because the teacher handed her over to Mr. Fisher, the school security guard. He gripped her elbow without a smile.

Uh-oh!

But the tall, bald-headed man merely escorted Skyler back to the gym. "When I was in school, disco was big." His voice was deep. "You know KC and the Sunshine Band?"

Skyler shook her head.

"Didn't think so." He pointed to the dance floor. "Now go out there and *get down*."

Skyler returned to the dance, joining a cluster of Fashion Club friends admiring one another's dresses.

"Great satin X-back."

"Cute bubble dress!"

"Is that hand-painted silk?"

Passing by a cluster of guys, the conversation was completely different.

"Give it back, loser!"

"What cheat code?"

"You are *so* fragged."

In the girls' corner, Madison made a splash in a dusty rose bustled ball gown. Her hair had been blow-dried pin straight, set off by jeweled earrings. Sienna flounced by in something ice-pink and strapless.

And then, the queen arrived.

Ashleigh Carr swept into the room like middle school royalty, carrying her silk, quilted evening bag like a bouquet of long-stemmed roses. A hush came over the gym as Ashleigh made her entrance. She was attended by Jason Traxler, a tall jock in a red rugby shirt, and Sean Burnett, a drama club star in an old-fashioned bow tie. A seventh grade girl trailed behind in a ruffled maxi-dress, probably ready to provide a lip gloss touch-up, if needed.

Once again, Ashleigh's fashion instincts were right-on. While every other girl had found the frothiest red or pink creation she could squeeze herself into, Ashleigh had chosen an elegant, white, tailored shift, with a single orchid pinned to the lapel. Skyler felt scolded by the simple lines of Ashleigh's outfit and the classic white wedge peep-toes that accompanied it.

Skyler's party dress suddenly felt fussy and childish.

While most girls had loaded their heads with combs, barrettes, tiaras, and glittery ornaments, Ashleigh had pulled her jet-black hair back into a perfect bun. Once again, she had ignored the trends in favor of simple good taste.

It was really irritating.

Now Ashleigh was looking up at the decorations, and Skyler could feel the entire room hold its breath. Would Ashleigh be charmed by the flickering candles and cupid cutouts? Maybe the streamers and lip piñatas were over the top. The queen slowly made her way over to the snack tables, and her eyes swept the candy display.

She plucked a red foil Hershey's Kiss out of a jar, tore off the wrapper, and popped it into her mouth. The room was practically silent.

Ashleigh paused. "This is so . . ." Everyone waited. "*Not* random."

The party broke into happy chatter. The Valentine's Day Dance had just been deemed cool, to everyone's relief. There was no need to endure it with folded arms and eye-rolling. Now everyone could relax and have fun — it had received approval from the highest levels of authority.

Maybe, with a little luck, Nathan would impress Ashleigh, too.

Skyler kept trying to circulate, but she was so nervous that she violated her own party rules. She had a long conversation with Jameeka about poof skirts, forgetting her Five-Minutes-Only law. Skyler drifted around the edge of the room, instead of the middle, where she would attract the most attention. And ignoring her Food = Boys theory, she didn't go back to the snack table.

"Checking out the guys?" Sienna winked at Skyler. Normally, Skyler would be scanning the room, deciding which one to target for the Sweetheart Dance. But she'd barely had time to look at the clusters of guys throwing candy hearts at each other. She hadn't even scoped out Kyle.

All she could think was: *When is the music going to start?*

Finally, Hunter Waxman-Orloff came out to the podium, and everyone applauded. She wore a red-and-white-flowered dress, with a silver heart charm necklace. She nodded, smiled, pulled off her glasses, and then put them back on again. Even *she* seemed nervous.

"As head of the Student Planning Council, it's my pleasure to welcome everyone to the Valentine's Day Dance." She looked around. "Yesterday this place was filled with dirty tube socks and lopsided dodgeballs; today it's an enchanted wonderland. Let's hear it for the *Decorations Committee!*"

Thunderous applause followed, and when it died down Hunter continued. "Check out the Walk of Hearts, the Hershey Kiss Candy Guess, and the

Cupid Sign-in Board. And most of all, stick around till the end of the night for the big Sweetheart Dance, when girls ask guys." Hunter smiled slyly. Skyler looked at Julia and held up crossed fingers. The girls giggled and the boys shoved each other.

"And now, get ready for a huge treat." Hunter smiled at the restless crowd. People were yelling for the music to begin. "I'm thrilled to introduce this year's band . . . THE VECTORS!" Skyler's heart was pounding wildly. She couldn't bear to look.

The curtain yanked open.

The five Vectors looked small on the big, bare stage. Nathan was wearing — *yes!* — chinos, a striped shirt, black jacket, and skinny tie. Huge relief. Absinthia was sharp in a retro men's jacket, Khalid and Melinger wore black T-shirts, and Jasper looked very 1980s Senior Prom in a powder blue tux. After they plugged in, there was a long peal of ear-jangling feedback. Skyler broke into a violent sweat.

Hopefully, that *wasn't* their first song.

Jasper stepped up to the mike. "Hello, Longwood," he said carefully. "Are you ready to ROCK?"

His over-enunciated way of speaking drew nervous laughter. This was the kind of moment Skyler had dreaded. She gave Julia a worried look, and

Julia squeezed her arm. Was he trying to be funny?

"It's great to be here." Jasper twisted a cuff link. "Sure beats the Health Carnival."

The audience shifted uneasily. Someone shouted, "Your fly's unzipped!" Jasper looked at his pants, and everyone laughed. Just a joke, apparently.

Not a good start.

Someone shouted something from backstage. "Sure." Jasper nodded at the band, and clenched the mike.

Skyler held her breath.

Jasper set the tempo. "One, two, three . . ." he said. "ON YOUR MARK, GET READY, GET SET, LET'S GO. . . ."

She closed her eyes in fear as the band kicked into their opening number.

But, wait. Was it . . . ? YES!

Skyler felt a surge of joy.

The song was a familiar hip-hop tune — last year's huge party hit, a song so cool it had kicked off its own dance craze. Who would have thought the Vectors even *knew* music like that?

The band was playing the same crazy instruments Skyler had seen in the garage: garden hoses, soda bottles, balloon-covered drums. There were sampled sounds, too — video game blasts and TV theme songs. It was a strange blend of melody, homemade sounds, and electronic beats. Their version was unusual, but somehow it worked. And it turned out Jasper could sing!

People listened with folded arms, skeptical after the awkward intro. But the oddball cover was strangely mesmerizing, and a few people nodded their heads cautiously. Scattered foot-tapping broke out.

Then the chorus started, and the song could no longer be ignored. People flooded the floor, drawn to the irresistible mix of danceable and goofy. Suddenly, the whole gym was jumping up and down.

Unbelievable.

The next song was even more outrageous — a pop hit by the same heartthrob the band had booed at rehearsal. Their version was so different — and filtered through weird instruments — the song sounded sincere and funny at the same time. So what if the beat was laid down by an electric xylophone instead of a bass guitar?

The crowd couldn't have been happier.

It was funny, Skyler reflected. These songs were mainstream, but the Vectors had put a different spin on them. Nathan had broadened the band's appeal, while continuing to work in his quirky style. Looking around at the jammed dance floor, Skyler thought it couldn't get any better.

And then, Nathan took the mike.

The full-body view was impressive. Tousled hair and geek-chic glasses made him look smart and cool. His shirt was sharp, his twill tie stylish, his unlaced high tops hit just the right note. A girl in a flutter-sleeve dress nudged Skyler. "Who *is* that guy?"

Nathan's smile was shy. "Greetings and salutations."

There was a murmur around the stage platform, where a few girls had gathered to scope out the band with interest. The cute drummer definitely stood out.

"Here is a song I'm not supposed to like," Nathan said charmingly, "but I do." After a crackle of feedback, Nathan adjusted the mike. "Sorry." He nodded at the band, and they struck up a funky girl-power anthem, made popular by a pop star whose tabloid life had made her a national joke.

He sang in a sweet, low voice, and Skyler got an unexpected melting feeling. Having a boy croon a teen girl ballad made the song tongue-in-cheek, but Nathan sang the song like he meant it. The band added water chimes and touches of electro.

The girls around the stage platform buzzed approvingly.

The pro-Nathan vibe got Skyler thinking. The change in him seemed deeper than a cool haircut and the right pair of chinos. Did he have more confidence or something? Skyler looked around the room for Ashleigh's reaction. The queen was holding court near the stage, tilting her head as she appraised the new lead singer. The jock next to her looked unhappy.

"He's adorable." Julia broke in to Skyler's trance. "And the band is great. Being a nerd never looked so cool." Skyler offered her knuckles for Julia to bump. In all the excitement, Skyler had forgotten to dance. She and Julia swayed back and forth, but her eyes strayed back to the stage.

Being a nerd *was* cool, Skyler realized. Having obsessions made life more interesting. After all — wasn't she was kind of a fashion nerd? Nathan pursued his hobbies more intensely than anyone she knew. What a contrast to Kyle, who spent free time pumping his muscles!

"I hope they give the band a break for the Sweetheart Dance," a girl in a pink halter gown said. "I see someone I'd like to ask." Skyler's bare arms suddenly felt chilly.

Skyler made up her mind. She and Nathan had to connect, even it was just a wink or wave. All she needed was a little sign that despite their falling-out, he didn't totally hate her.

She went up to the stage just as the song was ended. Nathan wiped his forehead. Their eyes met for a second, and he looked away. No nod or goofy smile.

Like she was a stranger.

Skyler turned away, scalded. For a moment, she was confused — did he not recognize her or something? Then she remembered the unanswered voice mail messages she had left, and their last conversation. He was ignoring her.

Feeling her stomach drop, she sank onto a chair in the back of the room. Against all odds, she had turned a Mathlete into a genuine hottie. Six weeks ago he was invisible, hidden under polyester sweaters, a terrible haircut, and science safety goggles. Now he was downright handsome. Even if Ashleigh *didn't* ask him, Skyler knew she had transformed Nathan beyond her wildest dreams.

So how had she managed to win the bet — *and lose the guy*?

Chapter Twenty

"And in a moment, the event everyone's been waiting for . . ." Hunter drew out the suspense. "The Sweetheart Dance."

A murmur ran through the crowd.

"But first — mad props to my buds, the Vectors." Hunter glanced behind her. "*Way* to save money on instruments!" The crowd applauded madly, and the Vectors looked at one another and smiled. "For this last song, deejay Fortunato is spinning tunes, so the band gets to dance, too." At a turntable in the corner, the gym teacher nodded glumly.

The stage curtain closed behind Hunter. "As you know," she said, "this dance is special. Because this is where girls get to ask *guys*."

By accident, Skyler found herself standing next to Kyle Townshend. She nodded hello at the handsome jock, who was wearing a white button-down shirt and baggy khaki shorts. She remembered when he bragged to her during class, showing her his ripped abs.

"Oh, hi, Skyler. Sorry, but —" He did a lazy sports stretch. "I already promised Sienna." Kyle sighed, and patted Skyler's shoulder. "Next time, you'll have to be a little quicker."

Skyler's jaw dropped. As if she had even *asked*!

Any leftover crush she'd had died then and there. *What a conceited jerk*, Skyler thought. She was about to set him straight, but there were more important things to do. She left the gym to see if she could get to Nathan backstage; this time, there was no guard at the door. She wound her way through a thicket of ropes and costume racks. Through the curtain, she could hear the intro of the Sweetheart Dance song.

The backstage area was empty.

Some of the Vectors' instruments were around — water bottles, eggbeater, mixer, electric guitar — but the band wasn't. Skyler bent down to pick up a funnel off the floor, which had been stuffed into a garden hose. As she stood up, she collided with Ashleigh Carr.

"Sorry," said Skyler. "What are you doing back here?"

"I've got to find that adorable drummer." Ashleigh brushed off her white dress. "Before the dance is over."

There it was — the sentence Skyler had been waiting to hear! Nathan had truly arrived . . . but she had to find him. If Ashleigh didn't get to dance with him, how could Skyler prove she'd won the bet?

The backstage door opened, and they heard footsteps. Skyler and Ashleigh looked eagerly into the wings. "Hello?" asked Ashleigh. But it was Khalid, the wild-haired Vector who ran the control board, and Absinthia, the water-bottle player.

"Have you seen Nathan?" asked Skyler.

"Nathan left." Absinthia loosened her necktie. "I'm not sure where he went." She elbowed Khalid. "Am I too late to ask you to dance?" Turning back to Skyler and Ashleigh, she said, "Didn't mean to cut in."

Skyler stepped back, amused. "You got to him first." Khalid raised his eyebrows and smiled, as Absinthia led him out the door.

Ashleigh turned to Skyler. "Now what?"

The door opened again, and Madison walked in.

"Aha!" She pointed at Skyler and Ashleigh. "What are you guys doing here?" Her ball gown looked faded in the dingy light.

"Looking for the cute drummer." Ashleigh sighed impatiently. Skyler did an inner fist-pump. *Yes!*

"Oh, yeah?" Madison squinted at Ashleigh. "Did Skyler put you up to this?"

Ashleigh looked confused. "What do you mean?"

"You just decided to ask Nathan Stillman to dance," asked Madison slowly, ". . . *on your own?*"

"I didn't know I needed a permission slip." Ashleigh's voice was cool. She tilted her head and looked at Madison. "Come to think of it, what are *you* doing backstage?"

Madison backed away. "I, uh . . ." Her face fell. ". . . followed you here."

Ashleigh lifted an eyebrow.

"Long story." Madison's voice sounded strangely hollow.

Skyler met her eyes with a weak smile. Somehow, victory didn't feel as sweet as she'd imagined. Things with Nathan were so bad, he hadn't even stuck around to see her after his big success.

That hurt.

"So the drummer's gone, huh?" Ashleigh reached into her purse for a breath mint, then peeled off. Madison and Skyler were left standing together in the hall.

"I have to admit," said Madison with a grudging smile. "You did a good job with Nathan."

"Thanks," said Skyler. And where had it gotten her? She didn't even know where he was.

"I mean it," Madison continued. "He doesn't look like some geek who collects comic books."

Skyler's eyes lit up.

"Oh my gosh, Madison, thanks! You've just reminded me, I — I need to be somewhere," said Skyler, breaking into a run.

"Don't forget my after-party," Madison called out.

"I'll call you," Skyler promised.

Skyler's mother had been reluctant to drop her off alone at the Longbrook Inn. "Want me to come with you?" Her forehead wrinkled as a man with green skin and pointy ears crossed in front of them in the parking lot.

But Skyler shook her head. She had to do this alone.

Inside, the hotel ballroom was teeming with strange, costumed creatures: warrior princesses, drooling aliens, masked superheroes, and winged oddities. Antennae and horns abounded. Skyler had to walk carefully to avoid stepping on capes and tails.

"Free hats here!" Someone handed her a horned Viking helmet.

Skyler tucked it under her arm and walked down one of the aisles. At every table, people flipped through boxes of comics. Under a SPACE VIXENS sign, a woman in a metal bikini and high boots posed for photographs. Another booth advertised ALIEN RAPTORS. Long lines snaked around the room as people waited to have comics signed.

Nathan *had* to be here — but where?

Frantically, she plowed through the aisles. There were hundreds of people; how would she ever find him? She prayed he wasn't wearing a mask. She scanned the signs on the booths: X-FORCE. TEEN TITANS. DINO-BOTS. RAT GIRL.

Rat Girl!

As she approached the booth, she spotted Nathan immediately. He was still in his chinos and black jacket, paging through a comic book. She put on her helmet and tapped him on the shoulder.

"Hey, buddy, this ain't a library," she said, imitating a surly comics dealer.

"Yes, but —" Nathan turned around. *"Skyler?"*

He looked astounded.

"I was in the neighborhood." Her voice was shaking.

His eyes took her in, from Viking helmet to high heels.

"You're — I — wow." He shook his head.

"Can we go somewhere and . . ." Skyler looked around. ". . . talk?"

Nathan led her down the aisle to an empty booth. "Aqua-Hulk went home." He moved aside a crate of signed photos and they sank into empty folding chairs. Skyler removed her helmet and nervously shook out her hair. Nathan sat back and waited.

She had no idea what to say.

"You were amazing tonight. The band, I mean." Skyler twisted her bracelet.

Nathan nodded. "Thanks."

"I was wrong about changing your music." She looked down at her red satin evening bag. "Wrong about — everything."

Nathan just looked at her.

"Before we met," Skyler continued, "I made a bet with Madison I could turn a Mathlete into someone Ashleigh Carr would ask to dance on Valentine's Day. If I lost, I promised to drop out of the race for Fashion Club president."

Nathan swallowed. "Go on."

"She *did* try to ask you to dance," said Skyler, feeling a stab of pride, even as she winced at her own behavior. "But you had already left."

"So you won the bet." He shrugged. "That's good, right?"

Yes — except that she and Nathan didn't appear to be friends anymore.

"No." Skyler shook her head violently. "It's not. I'm the one who needs to change — not you."

He looked at her.

"Nathan, you're my hero." She realized how much she meant it. "You go your own way; you think for yourself. I've always just followed the crowd."

He cracked his knuckles.

"You showed me stuff." She looked at the floor. "Not having you around has been . . ."

A woman in a purple eye-mask interrupted. "You guys seen Lightning Lad?"

Nathan pointed in the opposite direction. "Over by Japanese Imports." He winked and turned back to Skyler.

"I do go my own way." Nathan leaned on the

table with his elbows. "But I wasn't getting any-where with the band until I met you. The new clothes and glasses and stuff . . . gave me a way in. It didn't kill me to get a better haircut. Now, I kind of — I like the attention."

"Well — gosh," Skyler said.

"I wasn't happy you lied about the demo CD," said Nathan, getting exasperated all over again. "You should have just *asked* us. But you were right about playing something danceable — 'Ode to Missing Dental Appliances' isn't right for a party. You saved our butts."

That was nice to hear.

A guy in cardboard 3-D glasses came up to the table. "You have Captain Radar back issues?" he asked.

"Sorry." Nathan shook his head. The guy walked away.

Nathan turned back to Skyler. "Maybe you weren't honest about why you started up with me." Nathan shrugged. "But I wasn't honest with you, either."

"Huh?"

"I agreed to the deal so the band could get gigs." He looked down at his unlaced sneakers. "Maybe I had other reasons, too."

Skyler saw Nathan's ears turn red. Was this going where she *thought* it was going? Her heart was beating very fast.

"C'mon," Nathan said irritably. "Don't make me say it."

She didn't. Their hands met on the table, knocking off the Viking helmet.

An hour later, they were on the doorstep of Madison's enormous house. Nathan hesitated before ringing the doorbell.

"You'll have fun," Skyler promised. "I called Madison and made her invite a few friends."

When they walked into Madison's den, they saw a group of people never before assembled in one rec room. Jasper was eating a pretzel, while Julia explained her dress to him. Khalid and Maya were playing Ping-Pong, and Melinger was handing a glass of punch to . . . *Ashleigh*?

Skyler thought Nathan's eyes were going to pop out of his head. "Explain?" he said.

"I told Madison she and I could be Fashion Club copresidents if we changed the tone and opened it up," explained Skyler. "Starting tonight."

Kyle Townshend came up and greeted them with a belch.

"Du-u-u-de." He punched Nathan in the shoulder. "*Awesome* tunes. Downloadable. Good for working out." He gave Nathan a "You Da Man" finger point, and went to refill his soda. Nathan shrugged, but he looked pleased.

"Rice Krispies Treat?" Madison offered them a plate. She had changed into her second outfit of the evening, a striped sailor top and suspenders. "Where were you?" she asked Skyler. "I was afraid you weren't coming."

"Took me a while." Skyler looked at Nathan. "But I finally got here."

The Mathlete and the fashionista looked at each other and smiled.

turn the page for more valentine's fun!

♥ Valentine stories from your favorite Candy Apple authors!

♥ How to throw the perfect Valentine's Day party!

♥ Activities, crafts, and more!

♥ Plus a sneak peek at the next sweet Candy Apple book!

Valentine's Day: A Personal History

BY Holly Kowitt

FIRST GRADE. Make valentine "mailbox" out of shoe box, red construction paper, and glitter. Students bring cards for every class member. Sign of love: hair-pulling.

SECOND GRADE. End of mandatory every-kid-gets-a-valentine policy causes drop in volume. Get boy "friend." Signs of love: arm-bruise, spit-wad, insulting nickname.

THIRD GRADE. Big discovery: construction paper folded in half solves "lopsided heart" problem. Pet peeve: chocolate cupids that turn out to be hollow.

FOURTH GRADE. Scented stickers. 'Nuff said.

SIXTH GRADE. The first year that valentines aren't bought by my mom in a pack of forty. Cut out phrases like FAR OUT and DARE TO BE BARE! from magazines. Valentines start to look like really cute ransom notes.

SEVENTH GRADE. Mysterious red envelope turns out to be from great-aunt. Card says TO A GROOVY TEEN-AGER. Eat pink frosting out of a can until nauseous.

EIGHTH GRADE. Meet cute boy on Wisconsin family ski trip. Flirtation over hot chocolate results in juicy first kiss on bunny slope. Die of embarrass-ment when I look up and see parents wave from chairlift.

NINTH GRADE. Valentines start to involve doilies, glitter glue, and rickrack. Have spa day with girl-friends; vow BFs next year. Definitely.

TENTH GRADE. Still boy-free. Try every teen mag suggestion: Make all-red meal! Send yourself flow-ers! Host chick flick night! Resent not getting day off from school.

ELEVENTH GRADE. Decide V-Day is for losers. Have Anti-Valentine's Day: wear black, listen to angry music. Call friends to say I'm boycotting V-Day, in case word hasn't gotten out.

TWELFTH GRADE. FINALLY HAVE A BOYFRIEND! We laugh at PA bulletins and share notebook doodles. Sign of love: homemade mix tape. Agonize over card options: flirty Minnie Mouse? Far Side cartoon? "Love" in seven languages? Recruit panel of experts to determine how to sign valentine: *love* or *XO*. Settle on "luv."

SOPHOMORE YEAR OF COLLEGE. Alone again. Honor Saint Valentine with heart-patterned boxers and a hydrating facial mask. At café, hear V-Day's Most Dreaded Three Words: "Table for one?"

JUNIOR YEAR ABROAD. Acquire brooding French boyfriend with motor scooter. Exchange "Cartes d'Amitie"; translation misunderstanding leaves him thinking I want to set his house on fire. Learn that in French "little cabbage" is an endearment.

SENIOR YEAR OF COLLEGE. Discover fat-free candy conversation hearts.

TWENTY SOMETHING. Meet cute drummer at "Battle of the Bands." Share bowl of chocolate-covered strawberries. Sign of love: He wants to hear about all my past Valentine's Days. . . .

valentines

BY Lara Bergen

When I think of Valentine's Day, so many memories come to mind. Of course, there was always the annual, *torturous* chore of deciding which tiny, preprinted valentine to give to whom. (Did I *really* want to give the "Bee Mine" one to the cutest boy in the third grade? Or was I being too obvious . . . ? Oh, the pressure!) Then there was the pulling out of doilies and glitter to make valentines of my own. Not for the whole class — that would have meant way too much work — but just for my family. And who can forget the whole carnation thing in high school — you know, where the "service" club delivered flowers to students in their homerooms. There were pink carnations if you were just crushing; red if you were — gulp! — IN LOVE; and some plain old white ones for "just friends." (My friends and I liked to save our hard-earned dollars for the M&M's sold by the marching band.)

Now, I suspect the club had two main goals in mind here, don't you? One, to raise enough money to throw themselves a party; and two, to get the scoop on who in the school liked whom. The bad news is that although I probably watched hundreds of red, pink, and even white flowers being given out, I never received a single one. (But I did have my share of cute guys share their M&M's with me, you should know!)

There's another Valentine's Day memory that stays with me, too: my mother's crazy decorating! For a while, I actually assumed that *everyone* celebrated Valentine's Day this way. Then gradually I realized that, apart from my house, this extreme level of decorating — from the red garlands to the miles of pink crepe paper to the ginormous heart-shaped centerpiece in the middle of the glitter-strewn table — was basically limited to the card store at the mall. While I don't know for sure what inspired my mom to go so far, I can pretty much guess what she'd say if I called and asked her. . . .

In those cold, dark days of mid-February, after all the Christmas decorations have been taken down and the snow is still there, but more sooty-gray or dirty-brown, who's to say that a big dose of hearts and glitter and doilies and pancakes spelling "I ♥ U" across your plate isn't exactly what we all need? And if, later that day, a bunch of kids at your school are going to be walking around with pink- and red-petaled tokens of each other's affection, it's pretty awesome to have such a love-filled start to your own day.

So thank you, Mom, for being *my* cupid. And Happy Valentine's Day!

check out Lara's sweet candy Apple books!

True Luv

Laura Dower

I'm not sure Valentine's Day is fair. Yeah, it's all about too-good-to-be-true love and candy hearts and chocolate dreams and blah, blah, blah. But I can tell you that I've spent way more Valentine's Days angry because I had *no* secret admirers. I even remember getting accidentally left out of a "mandatory" classroom valentine project in fourth grade. Everyone got a card except for me! The teacher tried to cover for the situation, but it didn't help. I was the Valentine's Day Loser. Branded. Named. Done.

A few years passed. My mom remarried. We moved to New York City. And then, the unthinkable happened: I got my first *real* valentine.

One day, my stepdad came home from his office with his brows deeply creased. He always got that look when he was a) peeved, b) hungry, or c) embarrassed. In this case, he was c) embarrassed — *very*. He quietly told me that his assistant had been going through his mail at work, when she found something that was addressed to me.

Me?

Apparently, the letter had caused quite the scene at work.

From his briefcase, he then sheepishly produced a pale blue airmail envelope decorated with lips, SWAKs, and a postmark from Great Britain. My knees buckled. My eyes watered. I was surprised and embarrassed and totally floored. But mostly, I was flutteringly, achingly, and now *officially* in "like" with an actual boy who liked me right back.

Here was the proof.

Earlier the previous year, I'd gone to London with my parents where we dined with clients. One of those clients had three sons. They were sweet, tall, and had the killer accents to boot. One of these boys, the youngest one, named David, and I became pen pals. He sent most letters to our apartment, but he sent the valentine to my step-dad's office. (Why? Probably because he lost the other address! You know how boys can be.)

Inside my first "real" valentine, David wrote, "Postie! Postie! Send this quick! Or my true luv will be sick!" I fixated on the words "true luv" and his bravery for putting that into writing.

After that note, we wrote for years, and visited

back and forth, too. But the valentine was always the highlight. It's saved in an old soap box that smells like jasmine, and reminds me of how it feels to have my heart leap because of a few simple words sent across the Atlantic Ocean.

In the years since, I found the best valentines of all, my husband and my three children. But I will always treasure the embarrassing airmail and David, the one boy in the world who said I was his "true luv" when I was convinced I was "un-luv-able."

To Candy Apple readers everywhere, I share my "true luv" with YOU.

Check out Laura's sweet Candy Apple book!

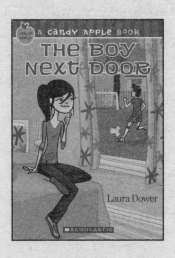

the valentine's Day That changed everything

by erin Downing

Twenty-three limp carnations lay on my homeroom teacher's desk, the bright yellow ones brown around the edges. It was Valentine's Day in seventh grade, and I was sitting in the back row of Mr. P's classroom wearing a black T-shirt and a grumpy scowl.

The flowers weren't helping my rotten mood. Our school did this dopey fund-raiser every year where the suckers who still believed in Valentine's Day magic could buy flower-grams and send them to their friends. I had never received a single flower, because everyone knew I hated Valentine's Day.

I had a real Valentine's Day losing streak going. Here's how February 14 had shaken out in the Life of Me:

First Grade: The dentist filled my fourth cavity and told me to lay off the sweets. My mom made me dump my box of sugary hearts into the candy bowl at the receptionist's desk on the way out.

Second Grade: During reading period, everyone went around the classroom and dropped cards and candy into specially decorated boxes on each kid's desk. Everyone except me, because I forgot my bag of chocolates and cards on the floor of the school bus that morning. Because I didn't have anything to share with my classmates, I wasn't allowed to participate in the valentine exchange. The "Erin" box came home with me, empty.

Third Grade: My pet goldfish died. On Valentine's Day.

Fourth Grade: The boy I liked told me my hair looked like a bird's nest.

Fifth Grade: I got a haircut and became the victim of a perm-gone-wrong. Now my hair looked like a squirrel's nest.

Sixth Grade: My grandma came to visit the day before Valentine's Day, and brought me an ugly turtleneck with embroidered pink hearts and a large appliqué of a horse with a fluffy purple tail. I tried to hide the shirt in my drawer, but my dad told me I was hurting Grandma's feelings. That night, I wore it around the house and deliberately spilled apple juice on it. My dad got suspicious and made me wear it to school the next day, even though the horse's tail was all sticky and matted with juice.

So this seventh grade flower-gram nonsense was not going to cheer me up or turn me into more of a Valentine's Day believer, I reckoned. "This is ridiculous," I grumbled, pulling out my book. I didn't need to watch our homeroom teacher distribute flowers to everyone but me.

Mr. P started calling people's names, and I quietly mocked Tina when she squealed about getting a flower. But then, out of the blue, I heard my name: "Erin."

"Me?" I squinted suspiciously.

Mr. P was holding a pink flower out to me, and I shuffled up the aisle to collect it. Before I could settle back into my seat, Mr. P called me up again, this time for a red flower. Then a blue one, then purple, then one of the wilted yellow ones.

This is impossible! I thought.

I hastily opened all five cards, and saw that each was from a different one of my friends. They all said basically the same thing:

"Happy Valentine's Day — this is going to be a good one! Love," and they signed their names.

My friends — who had done this nice thing for me, even though I was a Valentine's grump — caused my luck to change. That was the Valentine's Day that changed everything.

It was in seventh grade homeroom that I became a true Valentine's believer . . . and it's been my favorite holiday ever since.

check out Erin's sweet candy Apple book!

First Kiss

By Jane Mason

I was always a bit of a tomboy, so boys weren't a big deal to me. They were usually more fun to play with than girls, and never said "I'm not your friend anymore" or marched off with someone new at recess for no reason. Some boys were nicer than others, or sportier, or cleaner, but other than that they seemed pretty similar. . . .

Until Henry Olsen sent me a giant valentine that he had made himself, and instantly emerged from the crowd as the sweetest, cutest, most adorable boy in the universe. Nobody else paid much attention to Henry, but his lanky stroll, his calm, quiet voice, and his dark eyes suddenly captured me. And apparently he kind of liked me, too, because a couple of days later he invited me to walk home with him after school the next day.

This was my dream come true and my worst nightmare rolled into one. I was eleven and gaga about this boy. I thought about him all the time and my notebooks were covered with Jane + Henry hearts with arrows in a rainbow of colors. I longed to talk to him, to hold his hand, to lean in, and . . .

Before the valentine I hadn't given a single thought to kissing a boy. Now I thought about kissing a (particular) boy nonstop, but had absolutely no idea how to do it. And looking like a dork in front of the most amazing boy in the world was a fate worse than Friday's mystery meat hot lunch.

By the next morning I was seriously panicked. Luckily, it was "library helpers" day, so right after lunch I found myself in the company of Wendy Morrison. Wendy was boy crazy, a genuine kissing expert, and (most important) the kind of girl who loved to give advice. The word "kissing" had barely escaped my mouth when she began to demonstrate. She closed her eyes, leaned into the air, and starting madly smooching absolutely no one, right there in the library. "You just have to get your lips to his lips," she said. "The rest is obvious." I was completely unconvinced.

That afternoon Henry and I set off on our first after-school date. He lived several blocks from school, down the several-mile-long hillside that, along with the largest Great Lake, made our town a tourist destination. We took the shortcut, following the semi-frozen stream down the hill and through the tall-enough-to-stand-up-in arched tunnels that carried the water beneath the streets. The tunnels were cold and echoey and, in certain places, dark. I was so busy focusing on the barely visible ice beneath my feet that I didn't notice Henry had stopped and turned around.

When I looked up his face was right in front of mine, and I could smell his grape bubble gum. He leaned in quickly, his lips brushing against mine for less than two seconds — the best two seconds of my eleven-year-old life. Then he reached for my hand. "Be careful here," he said as we moved forward together through the tunnel. "The ice is really slippery."

Check out Jane's sweet Candy Apple books!

Chocolate Bacon

BY Mimi McCoy

It was my first year away at college, and my boy-friend and I had been together for only a few weeks, when Valentine's Day snuck up on me. I hadn't given the holiday much thought, but suddenly it was just a day away and I realized I didn't have a gift for my new sweetheart. What's more, I had no idea what to give him. A card seemed too boring, a box of chocolates seemed too extravagant — after all, we'd only been going out a few weeks — and anything else seemed just too risky.

Finally, I hit on a brilliant solution: I'd make something for him. It would show him that I cared without looking like I'd gone totally overboard. My boyfriend had once told me about a fancy, designer candy bar he'd tasted on a trip to New York City. It was chocolate with teeny, tiny bits of bacon in it, and he told me it was one of the most delicious things he'd ever eaten. So for Valentine's

Day, I thought I'd surprise him by re-creating this exotic treat.

My dormitory had a dreary kitchen that no one ever used, and this is where I brought all the ingredients. Since I wasn't much of a cook, I invited my friend Jenni over for moral support.

"Don't you have a recipe or something?" Jenni asked as I dumped chocolate chips into a pot on the stove.

"I couldn't find one," I told her. The truth was, I hadn't really looked. This was back in the days before everyone looked up everything on the Internet. And anyway, I had somehow come up with a very clear picture of how I thought this candy would be made. "When the chocolate chips melt, I'll chop up the bacon and add it," I explained. "And then I'll let it cool and harden."

The problem was the chocolate chips weren't really melting the way they were supposed to. They were sort of burning and sticking to the bottom of the pot.

"I think you've got the heat up too high," Jenni said.

She was right. Flames were licking the sides of the pot. I turned the burner down, but it was too late. The chocolate was now all clumpy and scorched-looking.

"Maybe I *should* just get him a card," I said, looking into the pot. I was feeling a lot less confident than when we started out.

"Don't give up. It just needs some milk or something," Jenni said.

"Milk with bacon?" I made a face.

"You're making *chocolate* with bacon," Jenni replied.

She had a good point. I got out the milk. While Jenni went to work fixing the chocolate, I started cooking the bacon. Soon the kitchen filled with the warm, comforting smell of frying fat.

The bacon was almost done when Jenni asked what we were going to put the melted chocolate in to make it into a candy bar.

I hadn't thought of that. I looked around the dorm kitchen, but, not surprisingly, there were no candy-making tools. Then I got an idea. "Maybe we could dip the bacon *in* the chocolate, instead."

"Like chocolate-covered strawberries?" Jenni asked.

"Right," I said. "Except it will be chocolate-covered bacon."

As soon as the bacon finished cooling on a paper towel, we got to work. I don't know how I imagined chocolate-dipped bacon could possibly be edible, much less romantic, but by the time we were done it was pretty clear that I'd made a big mistake. The bacon looked like a bunch of oily, oversized scabs that had been dragged through mud.

"You know," Jenni said as we stared down at the plate, "maybe you *should* just get him a card."

I was pretty bummed, but only for a moment, because I was already getting an idea. Maybe I could *make* him a card . . .

Check out Mimi's sweet Candy Apple books!

special Delivery

By Lisa Papademetriou

He's walking toward me.

Time seemed to yawn. My head felt light and people around me were moving in slow motion. I heard them talking and laughing dimly, and I could only see one person — my crush. Connelly McGreevy. And he was headed right toward me with a small smile on his lips, carrying a carnation.

He's walking toward me.

I'd had a crush on Connelly for almost two years. He was tall and had fair hair and blue eyes. He was quiet and sweet and his clothes were always freshly pressed. He smelled nice. He was friends with the popular crowd but still managed to be friendly to everyone. He came from a big family and lived in a huge house. I'd never had much hope that he'd develop a thing for a plump, smart-alecky Greek girl who lived with her single mom and had to mow her own lawn. Yet there he was, flower in hand. . . .

He's walking toward me.

Every year, the student council held a flower sale as a fund-raiser. I never, ever got a flower. Years later — okay, this morning, about three minutes ago — it occurred to me that if I'd wanted a flower so badly, I should have just bought a bunch for my friends. Then they would have bought a bunch for me. That was what all of the popular girls did. I'm a smart person; I don't know why I never thought of that. But now I was going to get one, anyway, and it would be better than getting a hundred from my friends. . . .

He's walking toward me.

I felt my heart beating — it thrummed though my whole body. My hands were cold; my mouth felt full of fur, like I'd swallowed a hamster. Connelly stopped at my desk and held out the carnation. It was red as a beating heart. "This is for you," he said. Connelly was on the student council. I couldn't believe that he'd delivered the flower himself. That was gutsy. I looked down at the card.

Happy Valentine's Day, it read. *From, Tom.*

That's so weird, I remember thinking. *Connelly*

spelled his name wrong. And then I realized — the flower was from someone else.

Connelly was already walking away. He had to deliver more flowers.

I could still feel my heart beating.

It's amazing how they never stop, even when they're broken.

check out Lisa's sweet candy apple books!

Missing the Valentine's Day Dance

By Francesco Sedita

I went to an all-boys school. But Valentine's Day was still a really big deal, because we all waited to be invited to the neighboring all-girls' school's Valentine's dance. Every year, it was a big topic of conversation: Who would get asked to go? And who would they get asked by?

But the first year I was old enough to go to the dance, no one invited me. All of my friends were, including my best friend, Jerry. I was really sad about it but didn't want to admit it to anyone. When my aunt found out that I wasn't invited, she called me and asked me to go to Chicago with her for the weekend. I did, and I pretended like I didn't care about the dance and packed a bag and we flew to fah-reezing cold Chicago on Valentine's weekend. And had a blast! We went to the Art Institute, ate yummy steak dinners, went ice-skating, and saw a show.

But the whole time, thoughts of the dance

were nibbling away at the back of my mind. All the things I was missing: the sugary red punch, the construction paper hearts, the streamers! Everyone dancing and having fun.

That Monday, I heard all of the reports around the lunch table — Jessica DeRobertis and Bobby Parker kissed; the good and bad music moments; Ronnie Sanderson fell flat on his face in the middle of the dance floor, doing one of his freaky dances; Veronica Adler's dad insisted she call home every hour; and Tim Winkinson played a prank on his date and she got so mad that she left the dance. I could see how much fun everyone had. I was really hurt all over again!

Of course, life went on. The next year, I got invited and had the best time. And every other year after that, too. And those are some really fun memories. Like the year they had a photo booth and we all crammed into it for what seemed to be hours, taking silly pictures. Or the year that some people came dressed up in *Star Wars* costumes. And, of course, when the dance went semiformal and we all took limos to get there and then headed to Andy Horrigan's house for an after-party.

But here's an amazing ending to my sad memory of not being invited: I just became Facebook friends with one of the girls that we were all friends with in grade school. And after we were done trading e-mails about what we'd been up to since then, she ended her e-mail to me, reporting something totally remarkable and amazing: She'd wanted to ask me to the Valentine's dance that first year. And was too embarrassed to ask!

I couldn't believe it.

I sent her a dozen red roses on Facebook. And told her that she made my day. And that we should be valentines forever.

check out Francesco's sweet candy Apple books!

Saint Valentine

By Sarah Hines Stephens

Nobody knows for certain why Saint Valentine was beheaded in ancient Rome. Some say he was performing Christian weddings. Others hold that he did not bow and scrape enough to please the emperor, but whatever the reason, my sixth-grade self wished that the martyr had died without the fuss, and had never been granted sainthood, because for me, and for many other middle-schoolers, Valentine's Day was more curse than blessing.

The ritual torture began each year with the construction of giant heart envelopes. The doily-covered collection baskets we were forced to strap to the front of our desks were designed to hold the valentines you (might) get from your classmates. And they revealed all about your social status. A too-big heart (if you weren't Andrea Gordon) made you look greedy and hopeful. A too-small heart (like Clint Borga's) was pathetic. Thankfully, Ms. Loughmiller liked to do things differently. She passed out thirty empty tissue boxes to be wrapped and glittered — all the same size. I preferred these more private receptacles instantly. The slot at the top worked well to hide the number of valentines inside and my best friend and I quickly found that if you wedged the last card in kind of sideways it made it look like the box was crammed full. Best of all, the slot kept nosy girls, like Eva Lizer, from being able to see if the love of my life, Sean Ghast, had slipped me a coveted Han Solo or a boring "You R2 Good For Me" valentine from his Safeway *Star Wars* box.

I usually resisted checking valentines at recess, preferring to open them at home, in private, so that the joy or humiliation of the moment was mine alone. Sorting valentines was like sorting Halloween loot, only there was a lot less sugar. One box of conversation hearts was all I had to get me through the heart-pounding search for the sought-after valentine . . . and heartbreaking reality that I had only gotten twenty-nine cards from my thirty classmates — shorted in spite of Ms. Loughmiller's instruction to give one valentine to every student. And the missing note was the only one I really cared about getting . . . Sean's.

I cursed Saint Valentine and stomped my box. There was no way a man who rubbed sixth grade girls' faces in the fact that their crushes did not think them worthy of even a cheesy Lando Calrissian, or that extra "teacher" valentine, rated a spot in heaven! No. He deserved to go someplace much, much hotter. If not for Saint V's lame day I might have been able to go on thinking that Sean sat behind me in science class for a better reason than my help on nitrogen cycle work sheets.

I was on the verge of a full chocolate meltdown when I spotted a small bit of white peeking from the box beneath my feet. I ripped open the envelope and my heart swelled and as I read: "You're the Obi-Wan For Me." It was signed with an *X* and an *O* from Sean. My crush was restored. And the martyr was redeemed. Only a saint could have created such a holiday.

check out sarah's sweet candy apple books!

CONFESSIONS OF A RELUCTANT ROMANTIC

BY ROBIN WASSERMAN

Here's what I want to know: Whose bright idea was it to create a holiday for people in love? A holiday that says, "Hey, all you people who are already wandering around starry-eyed and smiley-faced? Please accept our congratulations and this box of chocolate, because the universe loves a winner. As for the rest of you tragic little lonely hearts, lying on the couch watching sappy romantic comedies and waiting for a John Cusack / Michael Cera / Zac Efron of your very own? Eh, there's always next year."

As someone who has put in my fair share of couch time, I think I have every right to hate Valentine's Day. I should hate the cardboard cupid mobiles and the sappy Hallmark decorations, I should hate the Lifetime movies and the cheesy special episodes, I should hate the wilted roses and cheap carnations, and I should definitely, definitely hate pink.

I should, like a good little hater, hate the whole ridiculous thing.

But I just can't bring myself to do it.

Maybe it's because of the chocolate. It's hard to hate a holiday that revolves around chocolate. It's especially hard to hate a holiday that revolves around *receiving* chocolate. Boxes and boxes of chocolate. Even though the chocolates aren't usually very good, and most are filled with jelly or coconut or whatever that sickeningly sweet stuff is that's better left for the garbage. It doesn't matter: Chocolate is chocolate. And it would be easy to say I like Valentine's Day because of it. But that wouldn't be the whole truth.

The truth is, I'm a sap.

A cynical, sarcastic, romantic-comedy-mocking, secret sap. But a sap nonetheless.

The truth is, there's nothing I love more than those little cardboard Valentine's Day cards with Scooby-Doo confessing *"I ruv you!"* or Pikachu promising to choose me. I love the little stuffed bears dressed like cupid, and I even love those gross candy hearts with their cheesy sayings, despite the fact that they taste like chalk. I love each and every homemade card, and keep a collection of them in a shoe box tucked away in a secure, undisclosed location. The card from my little cousin, a nearly illegible crayoned message outlined by a crooked heart. The card from my best friend, who slipped it to me before either of us had figured out we would be best friends. The card from the just-a-boy-who's-my-friend-nothing-more-so-stop-asking — the card he always thought I threw away. (If he ever found out I still had it all these years later, I'd probably die of embarrassment, but I'm pretty sure he's not reading this. And there's no way I'm throwing it out.)

But here's what I love most about Valentine's Day: the possibility. The hope against hope that something unexpectedly wonderful will happen. That a secret admirer will leave you a flower, or the boy you suspected didn't even know your name will awkwardly shove a box of candy into your hands, blush, and then run away.

The hope that this Valentine's Day, everything might change. And if not, well . . . there's always next year.

check out Robin's sweet candy apple books!

A Frustrating but True Story about a Mysterious Boy

By Eliza Willard

When I was in tenth grade I had a monstrous, soul-shaking crush on a boy named Seth. I thought about him day and night. Whenever I was around him I felt nervous and couldn't concentrate. It was torture.

On that tenth grade Valentine's Day, I went to school with a sense of anticipation. Would I get a valentine from Seth? Would I get one from *anybody*?

Sure enough, an envelope was taped to the front of my locker. I tore it open. Inside was a heart-shaped card with the printed words BE MY VALENTINE, signed, *S.*

I almost screamed. Who was *S*? Could it be Seth? I was afraid to believe it. What if it was a prank? What if the card was from some other boy whose name started with *S* — some boy I didn't like?

I had to find out who *S* was. But how?

I studied the card. That *S* was the only letter the sender had written himself. My only clue.

I needed a sample of Seth's handwriting. If his capital *S* was the same as the *S* on the card, I'd know it was from him. I decided to pass him a note in class. When he wrote me back, I'd have my sample. A foolproof plan!

In English class that morning, I tore a slip of paper out of my notebook and wrote, *Have you started your history paper yet?* Seth peeked at the paper, and then scribbled something down. My plan was working! He passed the note back.

No, it said. *Have you?*

He didn't use the letter *S*! I tried again. I hated to play dumb, but desperate times call for desperate measures. So I scrawled, *Who wrote Romeo and Juliet again? I forgot.*

He wrote back, *Dunno*.

Rats! Was he teasing me on purpose?

Now I really *was* desperate. I resorted to theft.

When class was over, Seth went to the front of the room to talk to the teacher. As soon as he turned his back, I snatched an old English paper out of his notebook and slipped away.

Alone at my locker, I compared the *S* on the valentine with the *S*'s on Seth's paper. Were they the same? Did he put a curl at the top? Was it a printed *S* or cursive *S*? It was hard to be certain. After all, there are only so many ways to write the letter *S*.

Close enough, I decided. *It's from him.*

But if the card was from Seth, why all the mystery? What good was getting a valentine from someone who wouldn't admit to sending it?

Seth never said a word. And no one else did, either. It drove me crazy!

Finally, a month later, I got a big hint. Seth called me up and asked me out on my very first date! That was even better than a valentine.

We went through a few ups and downs and ended up being friends. Years later, I went home for my high school reunion. I found that old valentine in my dresser drawer, where I'd carefully saved it. I took it to my reunion dinner and showed it to Seth. "Come on, admit it," I said. "You sent me this, didn't you? Is this your handwriting?"

He just smiled and shrugged. "Sorry, I can't remember," he said in a teasing way that suggested he remembered perfectly well. "That was way back in tenth grade." I wanted to slug him. He was a very frustrating boy. Cute, but frustrating. And apparently, he never grew out of it.

check out Eliza's sweet candy Apple book!

♥

want to make this valentine's day
sweeter than ever?
throw a party!

♥

the following activities are
sure to add sparkle to your
valentine's day celebration.

♥

invite all your favorite people,
stock up on candy hearts,
and let the pink-and-red
extravaganza begin!

♥

sweetheart sweet peas

Surprise your valentine with a gift that he or she can enjoy long after February 14.

Materials:
Scissors
Kitchen sponge
Acrylic paint
Clay pot
Plastic baggies
Potting soil
Ribbon
Sweet Pea seed packet

Instructions:

1. Using scissors, cut Valentine's Day–themed shapes, such as hearts and flowers, out of the kitchen sponge. Dip your shapes into the paint

and create a pattern on your clay pot. Let it dry completely.

2. Fill a plastic baggie with enough soil to fill your pot. Tie it closed with a colorful ribbon. Place it inside your pot.

3. Write a note to your favorite "Sweet Pea" and tuck it into the pot, along with a packet of seeds.

4. Tie additional ribbon in a bow around the pot and you're all set to give a great green gift!

From-the-Heart Fortune Cookies

Now you can predict what future Valentine's Days have in store for you! Write fortunes for yourself and your friends.

Materials:

Nontoxic extra-fine marker
Sheet of paper, cut into small strips
Rolling pin
Chilled store-bought pie dough
3-inch round cookie cutter (or drinking glass)
Sprinkles, mini chocolate chips, or colored sugar

Instructions:

1. Preheat the oven to 350° F.
2. Using the marker, write fortunes on the small strips of paper and set aside.
3. Roll out the chilled pie dough till it's thin, and cut circles with round cookie cutter (or drinking

glass). Combine the scraps, re-roll, and cut additional circles.

4. Place one fortune in the center of each dough circle. To form the fortune cookie, fold the circle in half. Pinch the very top of your cookie together, so it doesn't pop open in the oven, and then fold the corners in to touch at the center of the half circle. Gently press so that they stay folded.

5. Brush the top of your cookies with water, and sprinkle with the topping of your choice.

6. Place cookies on an ungreased baking sheet and bake in the oven for about 20 minutes, or until they are lightly browned. You should end up with about 16 delicious fortunes.

Autograph T-Shirts – XOXO!

T-shirts signed by everyone at the party make great take-home party favors.

Materials:
Plain T-shirts (prewashed)
Newspaper or cardboard
Fabric markers

Instructions:

1. Have your guests bring a prewashed T-shirt of their choosing to decorate.
2. Place layers of newspaper or pieces of cardboard inside each T-shirt.
3. With the fabric markers, have each guest write a short Valentine's Day message and sign her name on everyone's shirts.
4. Finish up your T-shirt by adding hearts or other drawings.

collage valentine cards

Materials:
Old magazines
Scissors
Heart-shaped hole punch (optional)
Glue
Blank cards or card stock
Pens

Instructions:

1. Flip through your magazines and, using the scissors, cut out interesting pictures. You can also use a heart-shaped hole punch to cut heart shapes with patterns. Clip any words that seem appropriate, too.
2. Glue words and shapes onto your card. Let it dry completely. If you want, mix 1 part glue with

3 parts water and coat your collage to seal it. (To do this, use a paintbrush that is flat and is about one inch wide.)

3. When your card is dry, write a note to your valentine!

valentine Nails

Prep for your party by getting in the spirit with heart-decorated nails.

Materials:
Dark nail polish and light nail polish
Thin craft brush
Clear top coat
Nail polish remover (in case of mistakes!)

Instructions:

1. Paint nails with two coats of nail polish. Let dry until tacky.
2. Select another shade of nail polish. Using the craft brush, carefully trace the outline of a heart on your thumb and fill it in. Repeat on each nail. This is easier if you get a friend to help you, so you can do each other's hearts.
3. Wait for hearts to dry completely and apply one coat of clear nail polish to each nail.

check out

Rumor Has It

by Jane B. Mason and Sarah Hines Stephens

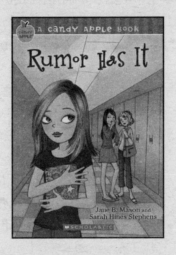

"She's probably in Slatt's class," Audrey said. Carmen shot her a funny look.

"You, too? Jeez, I can't believe how nutso everyone gets when somebody new arrives. I mean, she's just new. She's not, like, an alien or an FBI agent or anything."

"I know," Audrey said. And yet, for some reason, Audrey was incredibly curious about *this* new girl. If she had been on the cover of *People*, Audrey would buy it. Like everyone else at Humphrey, she wanted the 411.

"I think she sounds stuck-up," Elena Newbold offered at lunch. She plopped her tray down beside Audrey and Carmen.

Applesauce splattered from Elena's tray onto Audrey's hand. She looked around for a napkin to wipe it off and realized hers had fallen on the floor. When she sat back up the new girl was standing at the edge of their table. Audrey felt her cheeks get hot.

"Hi. I'm Mailee. Can I sit with you guys?" she asked.

Apparently she hadn't heard Elena's snotty comment. She smiled just a little and stood holding her tray while she waited for an answer. Elena was silent. Carmen was chewing. Audrey was having trouble talking, but she moved over to make room.

"Sure," she finally squeaked. In her head she was doing a little victory dance — thrilled by this unexpected chance to sit next to *the* new girl.

Read them all!

Accidentally
Fabulous

Accidentally
Famous

Accidentally
Fooled

Accidentally
Friends

How to Be a Girly Girl
in Just Ten Days

Miss Popularity

Miss Popularity
Goes Camping

Making Waves

Life, Starring Me!

Juicy Gossip

Callie for President

Totally Crushed